# Sir fartSalot
## hunts the booger

# and

# KEVIN BOLGER

RAZORBILL

# Sir fartSalot

## hunts the booger

A NOVEL BY
**KEVIN BOLGER**

ILLUSTRATED BY
**STEPHEN GILPIN**

**RAZORBILL**

**RAZORBILL**

An Imprint of Penguin Random House LLC
Penguin.com

RAZORBILL & colophon is a registered trademark
of Penguin Random House LLC.

First published in the United States of America by Razorbill,
an imprint of Penguin Random House LLC, 2008

LIBRARY OF CONGRESS CATALOGING-IN-PUBLICATION DATA IS AVAILABLE

Razorbill ISBN 978-1-59514-176-7
This omnibus edition ISBN 978-1-98483-661-8

Printed in the United States of America

1 3 5 7 9 10 8 6 4 2

To Fiona, Kathleen and Adam

To Tiana, Kathleen and John

Long, long ago in the Kingdom of Armpit, a small realm north of the Dominion of Elbow, there lived a young prince named Harry.

Prince Harry was an only child, and his nurses and tutors said that was a mercy, for privately they called him the Royal Pain.

Harry, you see, was a naughty prince. He made bubbles in his bath. He loosened the tops on all the Royal Pepper Shakers. He teased the moat monster by throwing pebbles at it and making the moat monster think it was somebody else.

Harry's father, King Reginald the Not Very Realistic, believed this was all just a phase. He hoped that someday the prince would grow up to be a brave and worthy knight.

"Roaming the land on horseback," the King suggested. "Smiting giants. Rescuing damsels in distress. Now that's the life, eh, son?"

"Gimme a break, Dad," groaned Harry, who was much too young to be interested in damsels. "That knighthood stuff is so medieval."

The only thing Prince Harry showed any interest in was his practical jokes. And magic. He'd always been fascinated by magic. He'd even learned a few tricks himself by studying the acts of second-rate traveling magicians who passed through the castle. Not real magic, of course, which only witches and wizards knew. Just sleight-of-hand stuff: pulling rabbits out of hats, sawing people in half (which took a bit of practice), a little ventriloquism ...

But King Reginald was not the sort of king to give up easily. He got Harry a position as squire to a castle knight named Sir Bedwetter. A knight's squire is a kind of helper or flunky, like a caddie in golf.

Unfortunately, Harry was not very helpful. At tournaments, he would loosen the bolts on Sir Bedwetter's armor so his iron leggings fell down during swordfights. Or put grease on Sir Bedwetter's saddle. Or file down his jousting lance so it was a foot shorter than his opponents'.

Finally Sir Bedwetter could stand it no more and went to the King to complain. He stormed into the King's Throne Room, barging past the Royal Attendants, who said the King was busy with Affairs of State and not to be disturbed.

But when King Reginald heard what Harry had been up to, he put down His Royal Crossword and summoned the prince at once for an explanation.

"Well, young man," the King demanded, "what have you got to say for yourself?"

"Oops?" Harry shrugged.

"That does it!" steamed Sir Bedwetter. "He has disgraced the proud name of Bedwetter for the last time! I *quit*!"

"Please, Sir Bedwetter," the King begged. "Give the boy another chance ..."

King Reginald was desperate. There were only so many knights in the castle, and most of them had already tried being Harry's tutor and resigned under similar circumstances.

But just then, they were interrupted by a loud horn blast. The Royal Crier bounded into the courtyard, blowing into a long thin trumpet for all he was worth.

"Hark, hark!" the Royal Crier shouted. He blew into his trumpet again. "Yoo-hoo. Hark, people."

"We're harking, we're harking," said the King. "What news have you?"

"A famous knight is come to the castle! They say he is the bravest and most famous knight in all of Armpit—though personally I'd never heard of him until a few minutes ago."

"You don't say ..." said the King. Already there was the gleam of an idea in his eye. "Tell us, who is this worthy knight?"

"They call him ..." the Royal Crier said, then paused to draw out the suspense:

" ... "

The King was on the edge of His Royal Seat. You could've knocked him over with a ton of bricks.

" ... " the Royal Crier went on.

The King frowned.

"Well?" He growled. "Out with it! What is this knight's name?"

"They call him ... *Sir Fartsalot*!"

King Reginald ordered a feast in Sir Fartsalot's honor, and when word got round, all the castle's usual work was packed in for the day. The cobbler and cooper left off cobbling and coopering, the blacksmith laid aside the umbrella he was forging, and everyone went home to get ready for that night's banquet.

No one was more excited than the King himself. He loved dinner parties. He spent the afternoon ordering the silverware polished and repolished, rehearsing the Royal Musicians, and threatening to throw the cooks in the dungeon if the soup was too salty, or if it was not salty enough.

The King, of course, had his reasons for making such a big deal of the occasion. He had an idea that meeting a famous knight like Sir Fartsalot, instead of the usual castle fuddy-duddies, might make Harry want to become a knight himself.

Nobody had actually laid eyes on the famous knight, mind you, for Sir Fartsalot had retired directly to his guest's chamber and spent the afternoon resting. But the palace buzzed with rumors of his knightly deeds:

"'Tis said that he slew the Tedious Boar of the Seatbeside Yew, the terror of all travelers."

"They say he calls his sword Lucille. A dragon swallowed it once in battle, and Sir Fartsalot choked the dragon with his bare hands until the beast coughed it up."

"That's nothing. I heard he once beat 12 trolls single-handedly in a fight."

"I heard that, too. Only it was a *dozen* trolls."

"You behave tonight, young man," the King warned Harry that evening at the Royal Table, while inspecting silver chalices for spots. "*No pranks.* And no cutting your food into little pieces and spearing it with your fork, either. Eat properly, with your fingers."

Harry rolled his eyes. Table manners may have changed since Long Ago times, but parents never will.

Sitting next to Harry, Sir Bedwetter was boring everyone with claims of battling dragons himself in his younger days.

"Rescued this peasant one time," Sir Bedwetter bragged. "Dragon had the poor chap cornered down a well. I still have the scars where he bit me."

"The peasant?" asked Lady Dimplewit.

"No, no, the dragon."

Sir Bedwetter took a sip of his wine, frowned at the taste, then hiccupped. Little bubbles escaped his lips and floated away.

Harry smiled. His powdered soap experiment was a success.

Suddenly, a loud wail from the Royal Crier's trumpet startled the King into fumbling a chalice down his robe-front.

"Harky, harky, everyone!" the Royal Crier hollered, then blew into his trumpet again. "Please rise for our guest of honor: Sir-r-r-r-r Fartsalot!"

A hush fell over the banquet hall. All eyes turned to see the great knight's entrance . . .

Well, it was a shock. Even the Royal Musicians slowed to a stop in surprise, then had to start up again in double-time to get the tune back on schedule.

*The mighty Sir Fartsalot was an old man.*

He was slender of build, white of hair, and hard of hearing. He had come to dinner in full armor, carrying his helmet under his arm.

The Royal Maître d' led him to his place at the King's table. The King himself held Sir Fartsalot's chair out for him. The old knight seemed embarrassed by all the fuss.

"We are honored, good Sir Fartsalot," the King said. "What brings you to our humble realm? Are you on a quest?"

"No, Your Majesty," Sir Fartsalot replied. "I am on a quest."

There was a polite silence. The King coughed and tried again:

"Tell us, then, what is the nature of your quest?"

"Yes, thank you, I could use a bit of a rest," replied Sir Fartsalot. "For I have journeyed long: over wind-blasted mountains and hurtling streams ... through dark woods and murky swamps ... in and out of moldy caves ... back over the same blasted mountains again ... "

"Got lost, eh?" Sir Bedwetter smirked under his breath.

Harry heard him and slipped half a shaker of pepper into his soup to improve his manners.

"You see, Your Majesty," Sir Fartsalot continued, "I am on the trail of a mysterious omen, a sign that some great evil is loose in the land. For many moons now I have followed this omen, getting sometimes nearer, sometimes farther, but never quite catching it."

"What manner of monster is this," asked the King, "that could elude such a knight as yourself?"

"In truth," Sir Fartsalot replied, "I know not what shape this evil takes. But by the signs I know it must be foul indeed…"

"You mean you've been questing all over the King's Acre for months without even knowing what you're looking for?" Sir Bedwetter asked in a smart-alecky voice.

The King fixed an angry look on him that shut Sir Bedwetter up immediately and caused him to take a sudden interest in his soup. He gulped up several spoonfuls, and Harry was pleased at their effect: Sir Bedwetter's face glowed first pink, then red, then purple … He trembled from his bald spot to his toenails … Sweat oozed from his temples … Tears welled in his eyes …

But Sir Bedwetter didn't dare spit out the fiery soup while the King's eyes were on him. So, with a mighty effort, he swallowed. Then he quickly washed the mouthful down with his whole flagon of wine.

When the soapy wine met the incendiary soup in his stomach, it created such an explosion that the force of Sir Bedwetter's belch lifted him clean off his chair, rattled all the place-settings at the Royal Table, and blew bubbles out both his ears.

Everyone at the Royal Table was shocked. Sir Bedwetter reddened, then scowled at Harry with dark suspicion, and finally hunched over his plate, pinching apart his dinner roll in a sulk.

The King glared at Sir Bedwetter. But he was wise enough to give Harry a warning look too.

Still, His Majesty would not be distracted from his plan.

"Young Harry here thinks he might like to be a knight himself someday," the King told Sir Fartsalot, getting right to the point. "Isn't that right, Harry? He's dying to hear about your adventures. They tell me you've battled every mythical beast from the Farfetched Malarkey to the notorious Crocapoop. Come, favor us with a few tales, won't you?"

But the old knight was too modest.

"I fear a lot of that gets over-blown," Sir Fartsalot said. "In truth, a knight's life is rather humdrum."

And no matter how much the King prodded, Sir Fartsalot would not be persuaded to talk about his heroic exploits.

When the dinner arrived, a hundred sumptuous and savory dishes, the King himself tried to spoon a bit of each one onto Sir Fartsalot's plate. But the old knight politely declined.

"Your Majesty," he said, "'tis a feast most wonderful. But I am afraid I must follow a strict diet for questing."

"Yes, we men of the sword must maintain our steely trim," Sir Bedwetter agreed, buttering his fifth croissant. "Why, give me a simple meal of wild game and ferns over this fancy castle fare any day."

"As for myself," Sir Fartsalot said, "I take all my nourishment from the wholesome turnip."

Everyone at the Royal Table was shocked.

"*Turnips*?!"

"What, for every meal?"

"Doesn't that get terribly boring?"

"Not at all," Sir Fartsalot assured them. "One may enjoy the turnip boiled, broiled, baked, barbecued, buttered, battered, breaded, blanched, blackened, basted, braised … And then of course there's turnip soup, turnip stew…"

Sir Fartsalot reached into his helmet, which everyone now saw was full of raw turnips. He held one up for all to see, then chomped into it with demonstrative relish.

"Turnips *tartare*," he explained, between crunches.

Sir Fartsalot gulped the raw turnip down in a few bites. Then he chose another and set this one alight in a candle flame.

"Turnips *flambé*," he announced, and bit right into the flaming root vegetable. There was a sizzle and a smell of singed moustaches.

The King summoned the Royal Waiters with a clap.

"You heard our honored guest," he barked. "Take this slop away! Turnips for one and all! And be quick about it, too, or I'll have you clapped in irons and vexed with feather dusters."

In no time at all, the great feast was removed from the

14

tables and replaced with plates of turnips tartare, turnips flambé, and whatever other turnip dishes the Royal Cooks could prepare in haste.

All over the Great Hall, people dined on hard raw turnips, chipping tiny nibbles off using their knives as picks. Sir Bedwetter tried to bite into his heartily like Sir Fartsalot had, but only got his false teeth wedged like a sword in a stone. Nobody else ate with much gusto.

Except Sir Fartsalot. He polished off several turnips in the time it took Sir Bedwetter to extricate his dentures. Then he sat back in his chair, licking his lips in satisfaction.

But he wasn't able to relax for long.

For suddenly a horrible smell filled the room. They noticed it first at the Royal Table, but soon it crept throughout the Great Hall. It was a smell most foul. Most vile. In fact, it was totally gross.

"Alack!" Sir Fartsalot cried, rising from his chair and drawing his sword. "'Tis the Foul West Wind!"

"Duh wad?" people asked, pinching their noses.

"The Foul West Wind," Sir Fartsalot repeated. "Silent, but deadly! When it blows ill, some great evil is at large in the land. 'Tis this very omen I have followed these many months of questing. But still I have not discovered its source . . .

"Good King," Sir Fartsalot went on, "I thank you for your generous welcome. But I fear I must not rest in your castle while the danger I seek is close at hand."

"Oh, doe!" everyone agreed. "You muthn't!"

"I must set off again tomorrow!"

"Yeth! Yeth!" they said as one. "You mutht go ad wunth!"

"We respect your sense of duty, Sir Knight," the King said, clasping His Royal Hanky over his nose. "But we did have one teeny favor to ask..."

"Name it, Your Majesty," Sir Fartsalot said with a bow.

"It's about the prince..." the King said.

3

"I'm not going," Harry said the next morning. "You can't make me."

"Harry, to travel with a famous knight like Sir Fartsalot is a great honor," the King pleaded. "You'll see the world. Have adventures. Why, when I was your age, I'd have given my manservant's right arm for such a chance!"

"So you go, then," Harry said. "It's your dumb idea."

They had been arguing like this from the moment Sir Fartsalot had agreed to King Reginald's unusual request. The King had an idea that a few weeks on the road with Sir Fartsalot would give Harry a taste for adventure and change his mind about being a knight. But the young prince stubbornly refused to go.

"Harry, as your father and your King, I'm telling you, you will goeth on this quest." (King Reginald always

17

slipped into the old formal speech when his temper rose.) "And you'll liketh it!"

"There you go again," Harry said. "Just because you're King, you think you can order everyone around. Man, I can't wait for the Revolution."

They were out on the Great Lawn, just outside the castle walls. Sir Fartsalot had not appeared yet from his chamber, but the stable hands were busy readying their horses. Harry's horse was a spirited mount named Wildfire, who already that morning had bitten the Royal Veterinarian, kicked over a statue of Harry's grandfather King Ronald the Insecure, and treed a stable hand. Sir Fartsalot's own horse Fealty, a dumpy old grey hardly bigger than a pony, was saddled, harnessed, and busy making a salad bar of the Royal Rose Beds.

A crowd of castle folk and peasants had come out to see the prince and the famous knight off. (Not, it must be said, with much regret.) Somewhere in the crowd, a small boy had run away from his mum. He was darting around between people's legs and showing off his mouthful of chewed-up gruel to strangers. His mother, a poor peasant woman, was at her wit's end chasing him. When a helpful monk tried to gather up the child, the boy just pulled the holy man's beard and ran away laughing.

"You cheeky devil!" the mother scolded. "Just wait till we get back to the hovel and your father hears about this! Now come back here *this minute* so I can change your bottom!"

"Poopy-pantses!" the boy announced.

"Hush!" his mother hissed. "If the King hears you, I'll *die*!"

"Poopy-pantses!" the boy repeated proudly.

He ran out from the crowd toward the drawbridge that spanned the castle moat, squealing, "Poopypoopy-poopypoopy—"

"Come away from there!" his mother shouted. "You'll fall in and catch your death!"

But the boy scrambled out onto the drawbridge anyway. He danced all over it, wiggling his bottom at his mum. Then he spied the heavy chain that raised and lowered the bridge and decided to climb it.

That was when the crowd saw the boy and gasped ... Not because the toddler had managed to scramble half-way up the chain—

Not because he was dangling over the castle moat—

No, what made the crowd's breath catch was what they saw rising out of the murky waters below ...

THE MOAT MONSTER!!!

That fearsome creature of the deep had surfaced right beneath the boy.

His mother nearly fainted from fright. But the boy only giggled.

Then suddenly, he tumbled from the chain—it wasn't clear whether he slipped or jumped—and plummeted into the moat below, screaming,

"Poooopyyyypantsessss!"

With a SPLASH! he disappeared into the murky water.

And then, like a bird striking a fish, the moat monster dove after him!

The crowd gasped. The boy's mother rushed to the King for aid, but when the monster disappeared under the water, she screamed and fainted at His Majesty's feet. Immediately, the King took charge of the situation.

"Sir Bedwetter," He commanded. "Get this woman off me!"

But then another voice rang out across the Great Lawn:

"Fear not! I will rescue the child."

It was Sir Fartsalot! (You had to hand it to him—he certainly had a hero's knack of timing.)

He strode across the Great Lawn to the moat's edge, clinking and clanking like a wheelbarrow full of tin cans in his heavy suit of armor. Alas, there was no time to change into his swimming trunks now! So from the rushes that grew along the banks, Sir Fartsalot plucked a hollow reed to breathe through like a snorkel, then stepped bravely over the moat's edge and sank beneath the water like a sack of stones.

The crowd rushed to the banks for a look. But the waters were a swirl of mud and murk. Nothing could be seen of the fearless knight in the moat's depths.

Only the violent froth and churn of the waters gave proof that a mighty battle waged below.

"Sir Fartsalot smites the monster!" the King decreed, optimistically.

"Are you kidding, Sire?" Sir Bedwetter said. "He hasn't a hope. That's the monster eating Sir Fartsalot and the child."

The boy's mother, who had just come to, let out another wail and fainted away again in Sir Bedwetter's arms.

"Nessie?" said Prince Harry, who knew the moat monster better than anyone. (It was forbidden to swim in the castle moat, so naturally Harry did it all the time.) "Gimme a break! She's a vegetarian."

In any case, Sir Fartsalot's struggle with that fearsome creature of the deep was the mightiest contest the castle ever knew. For years after, the story would be told of how Sir Fartsalot battled the monster on that fateful day. It would be said that he performed feats of arms unrivaled in the history of snorkeling. At times, he also used his legs.

This didn't come out till much later, mind you, because at the time there was nothing to see but a lot of splashing and splooshing. Indeed, for a while the outcome of the contest was most uncertain.

So when at last Sir Fartsalot rose out of the water as if by magic, alive and with the small boy safely in his arms, great cheers rang out.

"Hurrah for noble Sir Fartsalot!"

"He has defeated the moat monster, nasty child-eating bully!"

"Hail the brave Sir Fartsalot!" the King proclaimed. "He has rescued the little twerp!"

Even Sir Bedwetter joined in the great knight's praises.

"Not bad," he admitted. "Just what I'd have done myself."

Sir Fartsalot, with the boy in his arms, stood on the banks in a puddle. His armor was covered in clumps of moss and leaking torrents from its seams like a fountain. When he removed his helmet, he looked like a wet cat, his grey hair and mustaches plastered to his head. The loud, brassy croaking of a frog could be heard echoing from somewhere deep within his iron trousers.

"My little angel!" the boy's mother cried. "You're alive!" Then she added, "I'll *KILL* you! You gave mummy such a fright. Oh, brave Sir Knight, how can we ever repay you?"

"'Twas nothing, madam."

"Not you, you twit!" the King told Sir Bedwetter. "She means Sir Fartsalot."

"What do you say to the nice man in the tin pants?" the mother prompted her child.

The boy looked up at Sir Fartsalot. He stared at the

old knight's face. He pointed at something hanging from his moustache.

"Booger!" the boy announced.

His mother went pale as a sheet. "Bad boy!" she gasped, trembling in fright. "You apologize to noble Mr. Knight this instant!"

"I beg your pardon?" said Sir Fartsalot. "What did the child say?"

"Yes," bid the King. "Come again? We didn't catch that."

"Forgive him, O merciful King!" the mother bawled, throwing herself on her knees.

The King and Sir Fartsalot stared at her with blank faces.

There was a tense silence.

The woman looked to the crowd for support, but their faces said they were staying out of it.

Then, gradually, she seemed to recover her wits, and a change came over her.

"Er, that is ...*nothing*, Your Highness," she said, rising and smoothing her peasant's smock. "Just a lot of baby nonsense ... He doesn't know any words yet, actually." She lowered her voice and added, confidentially, "I'm afraid he's a little backward, Your Uppitiness."

"BOOGER!!!" the boy repeated firmly.

"Babble!" the mother explained, with an offhand laugh. "Means nothing. Wouldn't know what he's saying himself, the innocent babe."

She shot her son a fierce silencing look.

"Booger!" the toddler insisted. "Booger, booger, booger, booger!"

"Booger?" said Sir Fartsalot, who had never heard the term before. "What is this 'booger' the child speaks of?"

"Yes, tell us," the King asked, for naturally no one had ever used that kind of language in His Majesty's presence. "What means this 'booger'?"

"Hoo boy," sighed the mother.

Still, the crowd made not a peep. None of the onlookers wanted to invite the King's fury.

And so it fell to Harry, in a moment of inspiration, to break the silence:

"Why, father," he answered, "didn't you know that a Booger is a *frightful* thing?"

The King's eyes widened in alarm.

"Oh, yes, a *terrible* thing," Harry went on. "So terrible that mothers forbid their children *even to speak its name* ..."

Harry winked at the boy's mother.

"Yes, um, that's right," she said, catching on. "Hush, you naughty boy. Don't go *scaring* the nice people." And she grabbed her son from Sir Fartsalot and cradled him (or rather, *clenched* him) lovingly in her arms, with one hand clamped extra-lovingly over his mouth.

"What, you mean it's some sort of monster?" the King asked.

"Well, let's say a sort of 'monstrosity,'" Harry said,

his eyes fixed on Sir Fartsalot's moustache. "At least this one is. Colossal. Mammoth."

Naturally Sir Fartsalot was full of professional curiosity.

"Booger, you say?" he asked. "I don't believe I've encountered such a creature. Are they really as frightful as all that?"

"Repulsive," Harry said.

"I see," Sir Fartsalot mused. "And where might one find one of these Boogers?"

"Oh, you never know," Harry said. "Sometimes they can be right under your nose. So to speak."

Sir Fartsalot rubbed his chin in thought.

"Yes, indeedy," Harry added. "There could be one very *close to hand* all right . . . Say, you don't think there might be some connection—I mean, to the Foul West Wind and all?"

"Yes, yes!" Sir Fartsalot exclaimed, pounding his fist in his hand. "I *knew* my quarry must be nearby, for last night the omen was particularly powerful."

"You mean —?" said the King. "So you think it was a sign—? I mean, you're sure it wasn't the turnips?"

"I'm afraid we knights develop a sense for these things, Your Majesty."

"Galloping garderobes!" the King gasped. "A Booger! At large! In my own kingdom!"

"To horse!" Sir Fartsalot shouted—and clumsy armor and all, he leapt into Fealty's saddle in one graceful motion. "I must after the beast while its trail is hot!"

"Make way, people!" Harry added, as he climbed atop Wildfire. "You heard him. We're on the trail of hot Boogers! You remember, of course, that I was coming with you?"

"I don't know, Harry," the King fretted. "Maybe that isn't such a good idea after all . . . I mean, dragons and wizards are one thing, but this Booger sounds awfully dangerous. Maybe when you're a bit older . . ."

"Are you kidding, Dad?" Harry called back over his shoulder as he rode off after Sir Fartsalot. "I wouldn't miss this for anything."

And so it was that Sir Fartsalot and young Prince Harry set off to rid the kingdom of the dreaded Booger. Sir Fartsalot believed it was a quest that would make them famous in the annals of knighthood. Harry thought it would make them famous too—but in the annals of practical jokes.

The road from the castle led them here and there, but mostly there, and now and then they stopped at some peasant's hut to ask after their quarry. But the reception they got was always the same.

At one small hovel of mud and sticks, they came upon two peasant children playing in the dirt. The children, a small girl and an older boy who must have been her brother, were clothed in scraps and tatters and so filthy they appeared to have been dipped in muck.

"Greetings," Sir Fartsalot hailed as he rode up to them.

The children stopped their games and edged backwards toward their hut.

"Be not afraid," Sir Fartsalot assured them. "We come in peace."

The children stared back at Sir Fartsalot with big, silent eyes. The boy's face was grim and expressionless. But a tiny tear rolled down his sister's cheek, leaving a clean streak in the grime.

"What's wrong, child?" Sir Fartsalot asked with great concern.

The girl burst out crying.

"Do not cry, little one," Sir Fartsalot pleaded. "Tell us what troubles you, and by the might of our swords, we shall make things right."

She kept gushing tears like a fountain.

"Please, child, weep no more," Sir Fartsalot begged. "Hold your tears . . . Come on, stop . . . Oh, tell us, whyfor are you crying?"

"Your horse is standing on her pet stick," her brother explained.

"Oh," Sir Fartsalot said. "Sorry."

He reined Fealty over to one side, and the boy bent

and picked up the stick. It was broken in two pieces. Solemnly, he handed them to his sister.

"Poor Pokey!" the girl bawled, hugging the stick in her arms. "Killed in traffic!"

The boy put his arm around her shoulder.

"It's okay," he consoled. "You can share my clump of dirt."

"What are you two up to out there now?" shouted a voice from inside the hut.

A peasant woman poked her head out of the hut's door.

"Greetings, good woman," said Sir Fartsalot.

The woman stared in amazement. She wasn't expecting to find a knight on horseback parked in her front yard.

"A knight!?" she said, although that much was obvious. "Oh, dear! And look at the state of me!" She straightened her tattered clothes. She spat on her hand and smoothed a mat of filthy hair from her face. "If only I'd known you were coming, I'd have changed into my good rags!"

"Do not fuss, madam," Sir Fartsalot said. "We are but humble knights who seek your help in a terrible errand."

"Well, this *is* an honor!" she said. "We don't get many of your sort 'round here. It's mostly beggars and peddlers what pass along this road—you know, real *lower class*. Will yer grace stop with us for a bit of lunch?" Then, to the boy, she said, "Tom, go pick something nice from the garden."

The boy went and rooted among some rocks and stones piled beside the hut.

"But madam," Sir Fartsalot observed, "that is only a rock garden."

"Yes," the woman admitted. "Times is hard."

The boy brought his mother a large stone.

"That'll make a lovely soup," she said, turning it over in her hands.

"You are most generous, madam," said Sir Fartsalot. "But I'm afraid our quest is urgent and we must set off again at once."

"A quest, eh? Oo, how exciting! I suppose there'll be princesses locked in castle towers? And dragons to slay? And treasure?"

"We seek to rid the land of a grim and fearsome Booger," Sir Fartsalot explained.

"How's that? You'll have to excuse my ears," the woman said, digging wax out of one of them with a long, bony finger. "I thought you said something about 'boogers.'"

"Tea and crumpets!" Sir Fartsalot exclaimed. "You mean there is more than one? 'Tis worse than we feared, Harry!"

The woman looked at him sideways.

"Have you been drinking, Sir Knight?" she asked. "Taken a few too many wallops to the head, maybe?"

"Quick, good woman," Sir Fartsalot urged. "This is no time for personal questions! Tell us where we may find these Boogers whereof you speak."

"Where will you find—?" the woman muttered, then stopped and stared with her mouth open.

"Oh, *right* . . ." she said, pulling herself together. "*Boogers* . . . Now, let me see, where was it?" And while she was talking she glared at her children and made jerking motions with her head until they began creeping toward the hut. "Oh, yes, *now* I remember . . ." she went on, backing up slowly.

"Look!" she exclaimed, pointing past Sir Fartsalot's shoulder. "There's one now!"

Sir Fartsalot swept out his sword and spun Fealty around in one impressive motion.

"Where?" the old knight said, looking left, then right, then left again. "I see it not . . ."

From behind him came the sound of a door being dragged shut through sand.

"Wait, madam!" Sir Fartsalot pleaded. "Be not afraid! Do you not see how the Booger knows it has met its match and fears to show itself?!"

"Go away, you loony!" the woman shouted from the hut's tiny window.

Something dinged off Sir Fartsalot's shoulder and thudded to the ground. She had flung her rock at him.

"Please!" the old knight urged. "Be brave, I say! We shall protect you!"

A hail of small brown lumps splattered his armor.

"Wha—?? Pig droppings?!" he exclaimed. "Retreat, Harry! Retreat!"

They galloped off a safe distance from the hut.

"I see now how the whole countryside lives in terror of this Booger!" Sir Fartsalot said gravely.

Harry nodded, biting his lip.

But then the old knight did something Harry wasn't expecting. From his packs he took a knife and with it carved a small piece of wood into a rough, simple doll. He added pigtails braided from a lock of Fealty's mane, then tied the doll to a saddle pack that held half their food for the trip.

Then he trotted Fealty as close to the hut as he dared and flung the pack upon the doorstep.

"There," Sir Fartsalot said to Harry. "Pray the Booger does not return, and at least we have done what we can for these people."

6

Days passed, and their quest led them further and further from the castle. Nights, they slept under the stars, and mornings rose at dawn to breakfast on turnip pancakes made from Sir Fartsalot's own special recipe.

Then, shortly after eating, they would be visited again by the Foul West Wind, and Sir Fartsalot would take to horse immediately. So too would Harry, for at such times he found he preferred to ride ahead of Sir Fartsalot than behind him.

From time to time, Sir Fartsalot was called upon to perform knightly deeds along the road. Once, a frantic woman threw herself on her knees before Sir Fartsalot's horse, begging for help. But she was so beside herself they couldn't make out what the trouble was.

"Trapped . . . My Christabel . . . Oh, save her!" was all they could get out of her.

"A damsel in distress!" Sir Fartsalot said, following the woman.

But the damsel in question turned out to be just a cat stuck in a tree.

Still, if Sir Fartsalot was disappointed, he didn't show it. Instead, he went ahead and rescued the mewling maiden in true knightly fashion, charging the tree on horseback and shearing off the topmost branch Christabel clung to with one mighty swipe of his sword, which got her down in no time.

Further on, a farmer's wife begged Sir Fartsalot's help in chasing off a weasel that was at that very moment stealing eggs from her henhouse. Sir Fartsalot valiantly drew his sword and strode into the henhouse after the intruder. A mighty din of splintering wood and squawking hens followed, but in the end the weasel escaped with only a few scratches. The henhouse, unfortunately, didn't come out of it quite so well. And as for the hens, they suffered such a case of nervous upset they didn't lay eggs for a month.

Later they came upon a man whipping a donkey in the middle of the dusty road.

"You there!" Sir Fartsalot called out. "Why do you treat that beast so cruelly?"

"Oh, don't bother yourself about this good-for-nothing old sack of bones," the man grumbled. "I just bought the wretch from a lousy cheating horse-trader, but now it won't do a spit of work. Won't even budge. Well, by golly, I'll *make* it budge..."

He raised his whip to strike the donkey once more.

"Hit me again and you'll be sorry," said a voice.

"W-what was that?" the man gasped. The whip fell down by his side. "For a moment there, I thought—"

"I said, 'Hit me with that whip again and you'll be sorry,'" the donkey repeated.

The man's face turned pale as a sheet.

"I-I must be losing my mind," he said.

"Nay, I heard it too," Sir Fartsalot said. "'Tis an enchanted donkey, surely."

Actually, it was just Harry throwing his voice. It was a trick he had used all the time back at the castle, mostly for fooling damsels into kissing frogs that said they were handsome princes trapped by witches' spells.

"You see," Sir Fartsalot said to the man. "You never should have treated this creature so."

"That's right," said the donkey. "In fact, I happen to be a very powerful wizard who only took the form of a donkey for a bit of a rest. Now I think maybe I'll turn you into a cow patty..."

"No, please!" the man begged. "Spare me and you may live in peace in my best pasture."

"Hmm," said the donkey. "Maybe. But I think I'd prefer to stay in your house. The dampness outdoors makes my mane frizzy."

"As you wish, O great wizard."

"And I'll want oatmeal every day for breakfast," the

donkey went on. "Not too hot, mind you. And of course I'll need to sleep on your bed, but you can have the floor. And I find all this talking bothersome, so don't wait around for me to ask for things…"

**7**

**B**ut other than these side adventures, Harry and Sir Fartsalot made little progress on their quest. From time to time, they met travelers on the road, and Sir Fartsalot would ask if they had seen or heard of any Boogers during their journeys. Yet all his questions were met with the same reaction: The travelers would edge away from Sir Fartsalot and Harry with looks of alarm and quit their company in a great hurry.

"You spoke true, Prince Harry," Sir Fartsalot said. "So much do the common folk fear this grim and mighty Booger, they shudder and start at the mention of its name."

But on the morning of their third day out, they met a traveling jester. He wore rainbow-colored clothes and a cap with three bells on it, and he came along the road cartwheeling and walking on his hands.

"Greetings, good fellow," Sir Fartsalot hailed. "I see by your clothing you are a Fool."

"I prefer 'performance artist,'" the Fool said, hopping to his feet out of a headstand. "'Jester' will do, if you must, but 'knave' is pejorative. Anyhow, you're the one decked out like a bathtub with plumbing, so who are you to say I dress foolishly?"

"Ho ho," Sir Fartsalot chuckled. "I like this Fool. He has a saucy wit."

"I prefer 'piquant,'" the Fool said. "Say, did you hear the one about the knave who challenged the knight to a duel?" He produced a cigar from inside his shirt and wiggled it.

"No," Sir Fartsalot said. "What happened?"

"It knever came to knothing. Before the duel, the knave was heard to boast, 'The pun is mightier than the sword!' His King had him banished to the dungeon for it, and justly so."

Sir Fartsalot pondered this a moment with scrunched up brows.

"We have no time for jests," he replied finally. "We are on a grave and urgent quest. We seek a beast so terrible, many fear to use its name. "

"Ah, fear of the unnamed," the Fool said, "a common affright."

Then he added, "I see you are a knight of great valor and daring, but what if you hunt the elusive red herring?"

The Fool gave Harry a meaningful look as he said this.

"Herring? No, not a herring," Sir Fartsalot said. "The beast we seek is called…" he lowered his voice confidentially, "*the Booger*."

To Sir Fartsalot's surprise, the Fool didn't start or turn pale, as others had. Instead, he leaned closer to the great knight. "Did you say …" the Fool whispered, checking first over one shoulder, then the other, then both.

"Did you say . . ." the Fool repeated, with such an air of secrecy that Sir Fartsalot leaned closer, scarcely breathing . . . "BOOGER!?!?"

Sir Fartsalot was nearly bowled out of his saddle.

"I did," the old knight said, righting himself. "So, you've heard of it?"

"That depends," the Fool said. "Would this Booger be a large item?"

"Oh, very large, I expect," Sir Fartsalot said.

"Say about yea tall?" the Fool said, without indicating how tall that was.

"Oh, yes," Sir Fartsalot said eagerly. "Or taller, even."

"And about yea long?" the Fool said, without specifying how long that was.

"Yes, yes!" Sir Fartsalot said, growing excited. "I should think it would be about that long exactly."

"And would it have [*here the Fool mumbled something they couldn't quite catch*] like so? And an [*inaudible mutter*] like so? And would its [*something that sounded like 'toothbrush' or maybe 'cheese slice'*] be like this? Or sometimes, on the contrary, like that?"

"Why, yes!" Sir Fartsalot cried. "I believe you describe the beast to the letter! So you've seen it, then?"

"Nope," the Fool said. "Sorry. Haven't heard of anything matching that description."

Sir Fartsalot was crestfallen.

"But," the Fool went on, "If I was you, I'd follow that road there. It will bring you to the mighty forest of Knockon Wood, where shadows prowl, and perils lurk, and the trees whisper together in huddles. If it's adventure you seek, you'll find it there. But beware! For deep in the heart of the woods lies an Enchanted Forest, a place of dangerous magics, full of Bugaboos and Mumbo Jumbos and Things That Only Exist In Your Imagination. So mind you don't get lost.

"Anyway," the Fool said, hopping onto a unicycle he seemed to produce out of nowhere. "That's my advice to you, and you may heed it as you wish. It may not be very specific, but on the other hand, it's not very reliable either. Toodle-oo."

And he peddled off, weaving and looping, down the road.

"Boy, was *he* helpful," Harry smirked, as they spurred their horses on again.

"Yes, *remarkably*," Sir Fartsalot agreed, steering them down the path to Knockon Wood. "I say, though, did you happen to notice that curious steed of his?"

**8**

**K**nockon Wood was a vast untamed forest that ran along the wild western border of Armpit, stretching north to the foot of Mount Kaboom (the dormant volcano) and south into the crooked kingdom of Elbow. Harry and Sir Fartsalot reached its edges in two days' ride, then camped overnight before venturing into the great wood.

When they entered the forest just after sunrise the next day, birds twittered in the trees and morning sun dappled the trail. It hardly seemed to measure up to the jester's warnings, and at first Harry wondered if he might have played them a trick.

But as they rode deeper in, it wasn't long before the woods turned gloomier. The trees became older, taller, and loomed over the path with something like disapproval, choking out the sunlight.

Soon even the horses seemed to plod more softly, as if not to disturb the ancient hush. There was no other sound but the whispering of leaves and the occasional skitterings of Unseen Things among the underbrush.

Still, Harry wasn't scared as long as he stayed close to Sir Fartsalot. Somehow, just the sight of the old knight riding so tall and fearless in the saddle made him feel safe.

But once when Harry spurred Wildfire to catch up with him, he heard a strange noise, like a kettle whistling, coming from the old knight's helmet . . .

Sir Fartsalot was snoring!

Well, Harry didn't like *that*.

So he pinged him in the helmet with a brussels sprout from their food supplies.

"Alack!" cried Sir Fartsalot, sweeping his sword out as he jolted awake. "Show yourselves and fight, ye scoundrels! Who threatens the boy, dies!"

"False alarm," said Harry.

But for the rest of the day, whenever the old knight began to doze, Harry would bounce a vegetable off him, and Sir Fartsalot would spring alert crying "Alack!" and "Avaunt!" and "Á la carte!"

• • •

It was late in the afternoon and the shadows of the trees had begun to lengthen by the time they came to a little wooden bridge over a stream. And what they saw there halted them in their tracks ...

For across the bridge stood a huge, menacing knight. He was clad in black armor, carried at his side a tall black lance, and sat atop a mighty charger, also black.

The bridge was too narrow for them all to pass together. And this Dark Knight didn't look like he was budging.

"Hail, Sir Knight," the Dark Knight called out, in a voice like a grizzly bear taking its frustrations out on the tuba.

"What did he say?" Sir Fartsalot asked Harry. "I'm a little deaf at this range."

Harry, seeing an opportunity for a bit of fun, just couldn't help himself.

"He said," Harry explained, "'*Prepare to fight.*'"

Sir Fartsalot frowned.

"Good Sir Knight," he called out, "we have no quarrel with you."

"And I have none with you, fellow knight, both brave and manly," the Dark Knight replied.

Sir Fartsalot looked questioningly at Harry.

"He said, '*When I get done with you, you'll be begging for your mammy*,'" Harry translated.

Sir Fartsalot looked annoyed.

"Look, Sir Knight," he said bluntly, "our quest is urgent. Stand aside, please, so we may pass upon this bridge."

"*Me* stand aside?!" the Dark Knight thundered, and bullfrogs in the stream took cover under their lily pads. "Fluffenstuff! Stand aside yourself!"

"Look, Sir Knight, we came upon this bridge first," Sir Fartsalot said. "Thus I bid you, by the laws of chivalry, yield to us our right of way."

"I yield to no man!" the Dark Knight roared. Leaves fainted from the trees, and buds closed up in alarm. "Anyway, it was *I* who came to the bridge first. So I cross first."

"Are you calling me a liar, Sir Knight?" Sir Fartsalot said. "You insult my honor."

Knights in long ago times were awfully touchy about their honor. There was many a knight who lost his head (literally) defending his honor.

"Phooey on your honor!" the Dark Knight boomed. "Thou art a ninny!"

"Why, thou *meanie*!" Sir Fartsalot gasped. "Thou shalt feel my lance for that!"

"Oo, I'm shaking," the Dark Knight retorted. "Thou loser," he taunted. "Thou doofus." Then, from behind his knight's helm, he blew an enormous raspberry that echoed throughout the woods:

"Pb-btb-btb-btb-btb!"

"Villain! Bully! I'll run thee through!"

"Well, do it, then. What are you waiting for?"

So the two knights trotted their horses back about twenty paces from the bridge, then squared off and faced each other with lances lowered. They counted three and charged.

The Dark Knight seemed to glide upon his mighty charger. Sir Fartsalot, on the other hand, rattled like a pots drawer as he bounced along in Fealty's saddle.

But the old horse must have been faster than she looked, for the two knights reached the bridge at the same time…

*Clang!*

*Snap!*

Each knight hit the other square in the breastplate. Their lances snapped like toothpicks, and they were both knocked from their horses and thudded onto the bridge.

Neither was hurt. But they got up slowly, like two men completely encased in iron. With a lot of groaning, Sir Fartsalot managed to roll over and lever himself to his feet first using his broken lance. He swept out his sword and brandished it rudely in the other knight's face.

"Defend yourself, villain!"

Then the Dark Knight drew his own blade, and steel rang against steel. He was a mighty swordsman, but to Harry's surprise, Sir Fartsalot matched him blow for blow, and whack for whack, and wallop for wallop, and—well, you get the idea.

The Dark Knight twirled his heavy sword above him and brought it down with great force on the crown of Sir Fartsalot's helmet. Sir Fartsalot staggered, but didn't fall. Instead, he lifted his own sword and smacked it down on the Dark Knight's noggin. Then the Dark Knight took another whack. Then Sir Fartsalot. And so they went on taking turns like two kids on a seesaw.

You see, a knight in full armor was a sort of human tank. It was practically impossible to do him any real harm through all that thick iron padding. Swords and lances barely scratched the paintwork. There was only one weapon that really frightened a knight in armor . . . *The can opener*.

And now the two warriors dropped their swords and rushed at one another with a pair of these. Sir Fartsalot wrestled to unscrew his opponent's helmet, while the other tried to pry the old knight open around his beltline.

"Ruffian!"

"Trapezoid!"

*Uh oh*, Harry thought. This was getting serious. He had just decided he would step in and break things up before someone got hurt when—

Suddenly the grappling knights crashed through the bridge's railing and fell into the stream below with a mighty splash!

They disappeared under the water, still locked in combat.

Harry rushed to the stream's edge. But the water was a dark swirl of mud, and there was no sign of the two knights except a trickle of bubbles that was getting thinner . . . and thinner . . . then suddenly . . . wasn't.

One last bubble broke the surface and faded away in an echo of tiny rings.

*Oh, no*! Harry gasped. The knights would never be able to surface wearing all that heavy armor . . .

What had he done?!

How could his harmless practical joke have turned out so wrong?

And why was he standing around asking rhetorical questions at a time like this?

There wasn't a second to lose. Harry rushed to the river's edge and dove headfirst into its galloping waters . . .

9

And boy, was that ever a dumb idea. Harry's head hit the river bottom like a hammer striking a nail. Only he was the nail. He sat up, woozily, and rubbed a kink in the neck that went from his ear to his ankle.

Wait a minute...He sat up?

That's right. Harry was sitting in the stream. The rushing waters tickled him just under the chin.

Remembering the knights, Harry sprang up and splashed around in the muddy stream until he stubbed a toe on one of them. Then he reached under, gave a little tug, and both knights rose out of the water with another splash and struggled to their feet.

Each knight had the other in a headlock. The water came scarcely to their waists.

"I have thee, now, villain!" Sir Fartsalot announced triumphantly. "Thou art my captive!"

"What?" the Dark Knight protested. "*I'm* the one who has hold of *you*! You're *my* prisoner."

"Stubborn clod! Surrender or feel the wrath of Lucille!"

"Wait a minute," the Dark Knight said. "Did you just say, 'Lucille'?"

"Watch thyself," Sir Fartsalot warned, "for no man mocks the name of my worthy but somewhat effeminately named blade Lucille and lives!"

"I *thought* that's what you said." The Dark Knight suddenly relaxed his grip. "Farty? Farty, old boy, is that you?"

He took off his helmet.

"Sir Cedric?" Sir Fartsalot exclaimed at the sight of the other knight's red hair and moustache.

Both men became instantly jolly.

"Ho ho!" Sir Fartsalot said. "I bethought me thou wast some rapscallious villain!"

"Ha ha!" Sir Cedric said. "And methought thou wert a butt-headethed jerk!"

They tried to grasp each other in a bear hug, but only managed to clang their iron breastplates together like glasses clinked in a toast.

"Wait a minute," Harry interrupted. "Methinks memight have memissed something here. You two know each other?"

"Ah, where are my manners?" Sir Fartsalot said. "Prince Harry, may I introduce to you the bravest knight who ever donned the iron jockstrap: Sir Cedric Knotaclew."

"At your service, Your Majesty," the Dark Knight said with a bow.

"Cedric the Thick?" Harry said, before he could stop himself.

"Oh, you've heard of me?" Sir Cedric Knotaclew blushed. "Shucks."

Harry had indeed heard of Sir Cedric the Thick,

who was famous as the clumsiest knight in the entire kingdom—and the luckiest. He once freed a hundred prisoners from a dark wizard's castle, when really he had only stopped to use the toilet. Another time, he captured twenty bandits waiting to ambush him in a snowy mountain pass—by sneezing so loud it caused an avalanche that buried them up to their necks. And another time he slew a giant Scorpion with his bare hands—but only because he had forgotten his sword in his other suit of armor.

"Tell me, Sir Cedric," Sir Fartsalot asked. "What brings you to this wood?"

"I'm off to slay a dragon and free a bunch of princesses held captive in yon castle," Sir Cedric said, pointing off a ways. "Or was it yon?" He pointed the other way. "Oh, darn," he said, then sat down on a log and scratched his head.

"Actually," Harry said, "I think it's yon."

"Ah, right you are," Sir Cedric said. "Now I remember."

10

The knights decided they would travel together a ways, for old time's sake, and share whatever adventures fell their way. But evening was creeping over the woods, and soon it was too dark for dragon-tracking, so they stopped to make camp for the night.

Then Sir Fartsalot whipped them up a simple meal of tossed turnip salad, cold cream of turnip soup, and flame-broiled turnip steaks with a side order of seasonal vegetables (turnips). For dessert, there was turnip pudding.

There was plenty for all—and more than enough for some. Afterward, as they sat around the campfire, the two knights talked about their past adventures together.

"Remember the time we were trapped in a cave with that ferocious Whatzidoodle?" Sir Cedric Knotaclew began.

"Whatzi-*what*le?" Harry asked.

"The razor-toothed, dagger-taloned, long-necked, grizzly Whatzidoodle," Sir Cedric explained. "King of the Fancy Coiffures. It was half alligator, half eagle, half giraffe, half bear, half lion, and half poodle."

"But that's six halves," Harry pointed out.

Sir Cedric looked confused. He did the arithmetic on his fingers.

"Well, there were three of them," he said, and went on with his story.

Harry listened eagerly to these heroic tales of danger, for Sir Fartsalot never talked about that sort of thing. But then the conversation took an uncomfortable turn.

"Say, old chap," Sir Cedric said out of the blue. "You never told me the nature of *your* quest in these parts."

"Big day tomorrow, eh?" Harry quickly butted in. "Although I guess for a couple knights like yourselves, slaying a dragon is probably no big deal..."

"Aah," Sir Fartsalot said. "Prince Harry and I are on the trail of a fearsome beast that's been terrorizing the kingdom..."

Harry tried once more to change the subject.

"Tell me again how you braved death head-locked in the fatally smelly armpits of that giant troll, Sir Cedric," he said. "Now *that* was exciting, I bet."

"Terrorizing the kingdom, eh?" Sir Cedric said with great interest. "Smashing! I suppose it's left a path of destruction—houses wrecked, livestock gobbled up, that sort of thing?"

"Well, no," Sir Fartsalot said. "But people in the countryside practically jump out of their skins if you so much as mention the brute."

"Hmm, sounds promising," Sir Cedric replied.

"Say, ever notice how if you stare into the fire, you can see things in the flames?" Harry said, getting desperate. "See, there's a face. And look, there's a hippopotamus in a bikini…"

"So, what do you call this beast?" Sir Cedric went on. "Has it a name?"

"Boy, it sure is getting late," Harry said with a loud stage yawn. "We really should get some sleep."

"The beast we seek," Sir Fartsalot said, his voice swelling dramatically, "is the dreaded Booger."

Harry cringed. He hated to see Sir Fartsalot make a fool of himself in front of his friend. The truth was, he had grown pretty fond of the old knight, who was as brave as he was gullible, after all.

"The what?" Sir Cedric replied. "Did you just say, 'Booger'?"

"That's right," Sir Fartsalot said. "Have you heard of it?"

"Well, no," Sir Cedric stammered. "I mean, not—"

Harry squirmed as Sir Cedric fumbled for a reply.

"That is, only—"

Sir Cedric was flustered. Harry could see he didn't want to embarrass his old friend either.

"That is ... no," Sir Cedric said finally.

But any relief Harry might have felt was quickly snuffed out by the look Sir Cedric gave him. And what Sir Fartsalot said next only made him feel worse.

"I tell you, Sir Cedric, 'tis a joy to see you again," the

old knight said. "Until recently, my quest had led me such a long and lonely journey. Why, before noble Prince Harry here joined me, I had forgotten how much fun life on the open road could be. Now what luck it will be to travel in the company of *two* such brave and honorable fellows!"

## 11

They set off early the next morning in search of Sir Cedric's dragon. It wasn't long before they knew they had chosen the right path, for soon they came upon spots where the forest was scorched and trampled, as if by a herd of elephants playing with matches. Places where nothing moved or lived upon the carpet of ash, and nothing remained of the forest but cinders and smithereens.

A heavy silence fell over them as they rode past rows and rows of black stumps like the gravestones of once mighty trees. From time to time, the ground beneath their feet shook and rumbled like a cranky volcano. The horses grew nervous and spooked easily.

Before long they saw plumes of smoke drifting over the trees ahead. They crept off the path to get a first look at their quarry from behind some bushes.

The dragon was the fearsomest creature Harry had ever seen. It was as tall as a castle, with claws like talons, and teeth like fangs, and flaming breath that flamed like flaming anything.

"Flaming thunder!" Sir Cedric exclaimed with a whistle of appreciation. "That's a nice bit of dragon!"

"A marvelous specimen," Sir Fartsalot agreed.

"What is it doing?" Harry asked.

The dragon spun around and around in a flurry of flame and fury, in a gnashing, slashing, thrashing whirl of tail and tooth and claw and fire and hate.

"It appears to be chasing its tail," Sir Fartsalot observed.

"Chasing its flaming tail!" Sir Cedric said. "Well, I'll be!"

The dragon spun to a halt. What had been a dense thicket of trees was now a blackened pit of ash and cinders. And at its center sat the dragon, smoking nonchalantly and dreaming up new violences.

Sir Fartsalot cleared his throat.

"Well, Sir Cedric," he said, "as this *is* your dragon, I suppose you should get first crack. After you."

"Not at all, Sir Farty," Sir Cedric replied. "Wouldn't dream of it. You're my guest here. You go ahead."

"That's very noble of you, Sir Cedric. But really, I couldn't impose."

And so the two knights went on being terribly noble about it, each gallantly insisting the other should have the honor of confronting the mighty dragon first.

But at last, Sir Cedric said, "Go on, Farty, *show the boy what you're made of.*"

And somehow that settled the matter.

Sir Fartsalot wavered one last moment, then muttered, "Oh, all right."

He raised his sword in challenge, marched out from behind the bushes and roared:

"Ahem!"

The dragon dropped the boulder it was playing with. It landed with a thud that shook fruit from the trees in far-off orchards. The beast stared at Sir Fartsalot, tilting its head in curiosity.

"Excuse me," Sir Fartsalot said. "We are here to rescue the princess. Or princesses, as the case may be."

Smoke puffs curled slowly skyward from the dragon's nostrils.

"So, if you'll kindly surrender them at once..."

The dragon crouched over Sir Fartsalot, like a kitten about to pounce on a ball of yarn. It flicked its tail absentmindedly, and a stand of ancient oaks was whacked to kindling.

" …you will not be harmed."

In answer to this, the great beast reared itself up to its full height, spread wide its mighty wings, and shrieked an ear-splitting shriek that turned young warriors' hair white in remote villages. Then it stomped down again with a force that touched off avalanches on distant mountains and flipped Sir Fartsalot three somersaults in the air.

A brief intermission followed while Sir Fartsalot struggled to get himself sufficiently upright to resume his parley with the dragon.

"I must warn you," the brave old knight continued, when at last he was back on his feet, "if you resist, I shall have no choice but to unleash upon you the wrath of … Lucille!"

He waved his sword at the dragon in threat. It looked as teeny as a pin beside the beast's huge, scaly bulk.

The dragon responded by gathering in a mighty breath …

And blowing out …

…a fiery blast!!!

Sir Fartsalot was swallowed

up in a roaring hurricane of flame that went on …

and on …

and on …

… Until finally the dragon had squeezed out its last flicker of fire and sat back on its haunches, looking pleased with itself and panting a little from overexertion.

Where Sir Fartsalot had stood was now a charcoal pit of smoldering ashes. And propped in its midst was a blackened and lifeless suit of armor, smoking faintly from its seams.

*Sir Farstalot had been barbecued in his shell!*

"He's been scorched to cinders!" Harry gasped, watching from the safety of the trees. "He's been torched to flinders!"

"It does appear he's been incinamerated," Sir Cedric solemnly agreed. "Poor chap. I suppose he always was a bit flammable."

The visor of the torched knight's helmet fell open and hung by a hinge.

"Pfft … Pfft … Ptuh …"

Sir Fartsalot's face was black with soot and his moustache singed to stubble. But otherwise he was quite alive. He spat out a mouthful of ashes.

"Pfft. I repeat. Ptuh. Surrender the princesses at once or face the co-o-o-o-n-n-n-n—"

The dragon snatched Sir Fartsalot off the ground and dangled him before its deadly snout.

"—sequences," Sir Fartsalot went on, hanging by a leg. "I am giving you one last—"

Before he could finish, the dragon popped him into its mouth!

Sir Fartsalot went on issuing muffled threats from within the beast's jaws: "Mnn-hnh-hrm-hnh . . ."

Harry gasped.

"Quick!" he urged Sir Cedric. "Do something!"

"Er, I don't think Sir Farty would want us to interfere."

"But he'll be chewed to chunks!" Harry pleaded. "He'll be munched to morsels!"

There was a groan of twisting metal as the dragon worked its jaws up and down.

"Well, I don't know ..." Sir Cedric said. "It's against the knight's code, you know, butting into a fair fight ..."

Somebody had to do something—and fast. So Harry drew his own sword and burst through the trees into the clearing . . .

"Hey!" he shouted at the dragon. He waved his sword overhead, more in the manner of someone trying to hail a passerby than in threat.

The dragon stopped chewing and looked at him in surprise.

*Okay*, Harry thought. *Now what?*

Harry looked at his sword, then at the dragon, then back at his sword. He might as well have been armed with a toilet plunger. He was sooo dead ...

Truth was, he had never been much use at sword-work and all that knighthood stuff anyway. All he was ever any good at was practical jokes and magic. And in magic tricks, the key was always to divert the audience's attention ...

"Look," Harry shouted at the dragon. "Now you see it ..."

He waved his sword.

"Now you don't."

With a sweep of his hands, he made the sword disappear. (He had slipped it down the back of his shirt.)

The dragon stared at Harry.

Harry muttered some magic words and produced the sword, slowly, out of his ear.

The dragon's tail wagged slightly at the tip. Harry had the beast's attention, at least. That gave him an idea.

He held the sword by the tip of its blade and let the hilt swing back and forth like the pendulum of a grandfather clock.

"You're getting sleeeepy ..." Harry said, copying a hypnotist he'd once seen. "Verrrry sleeeeeppyyy ..."

The dragon seemed mesmerized by the swinging sword. *It's working*, Harry thought ...

But he would never know for sure. For at that moment, Sir Cedric stepped in front of him with his sword ready.

"Normally I wouldn't interfere," he explained. "But I suppose in cases like this, we knights ought to make exceptions where the safety of children is concerned. I just hope Sir Farty understands."

"Here, you!" Sir Cedric bellowed at the dragon. "That's enough of that!"

The dragon snapped out of its trance. It wagged its tail, focusing all its attention on this new plaything.

But first, instead of spitting Sir Fartsalot out, the dragon tilted its head back to swallow …

## 12

"DAISY!!!" came a voice.

The dragon froze. Its ears drooped.

"*Bad dragon!*"

A girl appeared at the far side of the clearing. She wagged a finger at the mighty fire lizard.

"Drop it!" she commanded.

The beast bowed its head with a guilty, hangdragon look. Its jaws slackened just enough that Sir Fartsalot was able to poke out of the side of its mouth.

"All right, you overgrown newt!" the old knight fumed. "You leave me no choice but…Oh, hello," he said, noticing the girl. "You must be one of the princesses. Have no fear, fair Princess; we are here to rescue you."

"*Rescue me?*" said the girl, who was indeed as fair and lovely as a princess, though more practically attired, in a woodsman's green tights and leather jerkin.

"That's right. From this dragon."

"You mean Daisy?" The girl laughed. "Oh, she's harmless. A little playful, maybe."

"You mean to say," Sir Cedric butted in, "that this dragon is *not* holding you encapsulated?"

"Oh, no," said the princess. "She's domesticated."

"Whether or not she's able to bear children is irreverent, m'lady," said Sir Cedric. "The point is, we were given to understand that this dragon was holding some princesses captivated in some castle or other, somewhere 'round here."

"Well, my sisters and I live in a castle back there," the girl said, pointing over her shoulder. "But nobody's holding anybody captive. Daisy is my pet. Aren't you girl?" The princess petted the dragon's scaly knee.

"Your *pet*?" Sir Cedric said. "Well I'll be flamed!"

"Be that as it may, my dear Princess," Sir Fartsalot said, still wedged between Daisy's

back molars. "Nevertheless, if your dragon does not unhand me at once—"

"I think you mean 'unmouth' you," Harry corrected.

"Er, right. Well, as I was saying, I shall have no choice but to unleash the wrath of—"

"Lucille," said the girl. "So I heard. Fine, have it your way." And in a stern voice, she commanded, "Daisy . . . *Drop it*."

The dragon let its lower jaw go slack and Sir Fartsalot fell on his head with a clonk.

Harry and Sir Cedric helped him to his feet.

Sir Fartsalot, dripping with dragon slobber, introduced himself and his companions.

The girl's name was Gwendolyn, and she was indeed a princess, though not the type to go making a big to-do about it. She told them she lived in a nearby castle with her sisters, Princess Guinnevere, Princess Gwyneth, Princess Gwizelda . . . and so many other princesses Harry and the knights soon lost track of names.

"'Tis lucky you arrived when you did, fair Princess," Sir Fartsalot said. "For a few moments later and I fear I would've made dragon nuggets out of this over-frisky 'pet' of yours."

At this, Daisy the dragon leaned forward and licked Sir Fartsalot's face with a wet, slurpy dragon kiss.

Princess Gwendolyn invited Harry and the knights back to her castle for lunch.

"But I should warn you about my sisters," she said. "You never saw such a silly bunch of princesses."

S o Princess Gwendolyn brought them back to her castle, leading Daisy on a leash and stopping now and then to let the dragon sniff or scorch things that caught its interest.

The castle, as they approached, seemed to be draped with all sorts of colored flags and pennants that flapped in the breeze. But as they got nearer, they saw these were really princesses waving silk veils at them from every battlement and tower window.

They entered the castle gates. Princesses fluttered into the courtyard from all directions, smoothing their royal gowns, and fussing with their tiaras, and shoving one another out of the way in a most unprincessly fashion.

"O Love!" sighed a princess.

"O Romance!" sapped another.

"Oh, please!" sneered Gwendolyn.

Gwendolyn's sisters huddled together in a phalanx of princesses, tittering like pigeons, making goo-goo eyes behind their veils, and nudging each other aside with an occasional sharp elbow.

"Helllllloooo, Sir Knights," they cooed, batting their eyelashes.

"I get the wed-head," whispered the princess with a lisp (this was Gwizelda). "Dat udda' one must be seventy yeahs owed."

"Get out," said the princess who was extremely bossy. "He can't be a day over sixty, and I say he's *dreamy*."

The princesses invited their guests to lunch, which they insisted on calling a "luncheon." They led them to the dining hall, where a long table was set with frilly placemats and fancy dishes.

Sir Fartsalot was seated between the princess who was extremely bossy and the princess who always talked about herself. For some reason he spoke very little.

Sir Cedric sat beside the princess who was into astrology. But fortunately the princess who never let people finish their sentences sat on his other side and kept cutting her short.

Harry sat at the end of the table with Gwendolyn.

"You princes get all the luck," Gwendolyn complained. "Roaming around, having adventures all the time."

"It's okay, I guess," said Harry.

"Okay? Huh! I wish I could live like that," Gwendolyn sighed. "Wild and free. Master of my own destiny." Then she added bitterly, "You ever try to get in the bathroom in a castle with 12 princesses?"

During the meal, Harry noticed princesses winking across the table at Sir Fartsalot and Sir Cedric, or blowing them kisses, or passing them secret love notes that made the knights blush in alarm.

After lunch, the princess who was extremely bossy sent Gwendolyn and Harry outdoors to play. They were glad to get away—but Sir Fartsalot and Sir Cedric watched them go with desperate looks ...

• • •

Outside, Gwendolyn and Harry played hide-and-seek with Daisy until the dragon went off in a sulk because it was always the first one found.

Then they tried their hands at archery, fencing with wooden swords, thumb-wrestling and dragon-patty tossing. Gwendolyn beat Harry at every sport.

"Isn't this fun?" she beamed. "All my sisters ever want to do is have fancy dress balls."

Gwendolyn begged Harry to show her some more magic like she had seen him do with Daisy. So Harry did some tricks with a length of rope. He cut it into tiny sections, then pulled it out of a hat in one piece again. He tied it in knots that came undone with a yank and some magic words. Then, for a finale, he made the rope dance like a snake charmer's cobra.

"Cool!" Gwendolyn said. "Watch me climb it!"

She started to scramble hand-over-hand up the levitating rope.

"I don't think—" Harry tried to warn her. But before he could finish, the rope collapsed, throwing Gwendolyn to the ground.

"Are you all right?" Harry asked.

Gwendolyn sat up with her hair in tangles and a wild look in her eyes.

"Do that again!" she said. "Wait, I'll get a longer rope!"

• • •

When they came back inside, the castle was dark and eerily deserted. There wasn't a knight or a princess in sight.

Gwendolyn led Harry to a gloomy upstairs hall where the castle's guest rooms were. The hall was in darkness because all the lanterns along its walls had burned out. Cobwebs stretched from the ceiling. Paintings hung askew.

"Sorry it's a little dusty, but we don't get many guests," Gwendolyn apologized. "That is, except for the ghosts."

"G-ghosts?!" Harry stammered.

The only light was a dim glow coming from under a door at the end of the hall.

"That's probably your friends down there," Gwendolyn said. "Or else it's the ghosts. Well, good night."

She clapped him on the back, jolting him forward, and left.

Harry was alone. He stood frozen a minute, listening for ghosts, then slowly took a few steps forward . . .

The floor creaked under him—which gave him an eerie feeling, especially as it was a stone floor.

Harry jumped as a rat scurried across his path. Then another, larger rat scurried after it, licking its chops.

Finally Harry reached the door at the end of the hall. He knocked three times.

*Tap—tap—tap . . .*

The light inside the room suddenly went out, throwing the hall into pitch darkness.

"S-Sir Fartsalot?" Harry called out in terror. "Sir Cedric?"

"They're not here," answered a voice behind the door. "They, er...left."

"Sir Cedric, is that you?" Harry replied. "It's me, Harry."

Behind the door, there was a loud commotion of heavy objects being dragged across the floor. Finally the door opened an inch. An eye peered out from the crack.

"It *is* you," Sir Cedric exclaimed. He swung open the door and hurried Harry into the room. "Sorry, Your Highness, but one can't be too careful around here."

Inside was a large, dusty bedroom lit by moonlight. Sir Fartsalot stood by the open window, keeping watch from behind a curtain. Sir Cedric pushed a velvet-covered sofa and half a bedroom suite back up against the door. The floor was littered with rocks and scraps of parchment.

"What's going on?" Harry asked.

"A siege," Sir Fartsalot explained. "We're completely surrounded."

His face, when he turned away from the window, was covered in red smears.

"Sir Fartsalot!" Harry gasped. "Is that…blood??!"

"I only wish it was," Sir Fartsalot replied bleakly.

Harry stepped closer and saw the smears were not blood at all, but…

*Lipstick!*

Harry picked up one of the rocks that were scattered all over the floor and untied the parchment wrapped around it. It read:

*My Knight in Shining Amour,*

*What happiness fills my soul, to know that we are in love!*

*Of course you couldn't come right out and say so, but I read it in your eyes, darling. I saw it in the way you looked at me. Or rather, in the way you didn't. In the way you turned quickly away whenever our eyes met, because you were so overcome with emotion. I could tell your heart thrilled as mine did by the way you jumped—actually jumped—when my hand brushed against yours as I passed the salt. (Now I shall wear that saltshaker next to my heart forever, as a symbol of our love!) And though you could not speak your feelings openly, I caught your secret meaning when you told me, "Madam, you are standing on my foot." O, what poetry those words were to my ears!…*

"They're all the same," Sir Cedric said grimly. "They've been raining in here like cannon balls. That one got me right between the eyes," he added, patting a nasty bump on his forehead.

14

Sometime after midnight the strain finally started to get to Sir Cedric. "I can't stand this waiting and hiding like cowards any longer, Sir Farty," he said. "I say we go out there and sneak away like men!"

So they dug through the barricade and bravely tiptoed out into the castle's dark corridors.

The knights slunk along, fearing princesses lurked around every corner. Harry kept close behind them, looking over his shoulder for ghosts.

They made it out of the guest hall . . .

and down the winding staircase . . .

. . . But as they were passing through the ground-floor library, a ghoulish figure appeared in the doorway ahead, barring their way!

It was more hideous than any ghost Harry had ever imagined. Wrapped in a corpse's shroud, it seemed to be made entirely of muck-brown bog, with swamp snakes in its hair. Sir Fartsalot raised his sword to—

"Oo, I thought it was you," the bog corpse trilled. "You were coming to sneak away with me—how romantic!"

It was the princess who never let people finish their sentences, in her dressing gown. She had her hair up in curlers and a mud mask on her face.

"My dear lady . . ." Sir Fartsalot began, and Harry heard the note of fear in his voice.

Suddenly princesses in housecoats and nightgowns poured into the room from every direction. Gwendolyn appeared too, curious to see what all the racket was about.

"I guess our secret's out, darling," said the princess who never let people finish their sentences, throwing her arms around Sir Fartsalot. "Sisters," she announced, "we're running away together!"

"But I was going to run away with him first!" another princess protested. "I'm already packed!"

"Ladies, ladies!" Sir Fartsalot said. "I'm afraid there's been a terrible mix-up. You see, we only stopped at your castle because we thought you were in distress."

"Oh, I'm in distwess!" Princess Gwizelda cried, pressing the back of her hand to her forehead and fainting at Sir Cedric's feet.

"Me too!" wailed another princess. "Help, help! I'm in distress!"

And then all the princesses but Gwendolyn flung themselves at the feet, and around the necks, and about the waists of their rescuers.

"Oh, save me, you big hunk of knightly beefcake!" cried the princess who was a little crass, jumping into Sir Cedric's arms and nearly crushing him.

"Let's ride off into the sunset together!" ordered the princess who was extremely bossy. "Fetch my bags, darling."

"Ugh! You shameless stereotypes!" Gwendolyn said with disgust. Then she turned and exited the chapter in protest.

Sir Fartsalot and Sir Cedric meanwhile found themselves backed into the most desperate corner of their careers.

"We're—awfully—sorry—girls," Sir Cedric said, prying princesses from his every limb. "But—we are— men of—adventure—you see—"

"So as—you aren't—in any—present—danger,"

Sir Fartsalot said, shaking a last princess off his leg and assuming a defensive position atop an old bookcase. "I'm afraid [*gasp for breath*] we really must [*pant*] be on our way. You see, we thought you were being held at bay by a dragon ... or some ogres, perhaps ... or at least a—"

"Ogres?" said the princess who never let people finish their sentences. "Well, why didn't you say so?! We've got loads of *those*."

"Why, yes!" the princesses cried in delight. "The woods around here are *full* of ogres, now that you mention it."

But the knights were skeptical.

"It's true! Princesses' honor."

"We live in constant terror of them!"

"So you simply *must* stay here in the castle," said the princess who was extremely bossy. "To protect us. From those frightful ogres."

But Sir Fartsalot was not prepared to come down from his bookcase just yet.

"I think rather we shall sally forth into the woods and engage them in battle right away," he said. "What do you say, Sir Cedric?"

"I agree, Sir Farty," he answered hastily. "Best spring on them while we have the ailment of surprise."

"Oh, no!" wailed the princesses. "It's too *dangerous*! Just wait here to chase them off if they happen to come along."

But the knights insisted. Sir Cedric said, "We knights *crave* danger!" And Sir Fartsalot refused to come down from his bookcase until the princesses gave in.

At last it was settled, and Harry and the two knights set forth in the dark night without delay. The princesses saw them off, sighing "Alas!" and alternately waving their veils and blowing their noses into them as they wept.

"Well, Sir Cedric," Sir Fartsalot said, when they were a good distance from the castle, "*that* was a close call."

"Right you are, Sir Farty," his friend replied. "I'd sooner take my chances with a band of ogres any day!"

# 15

The forests around the castle were damp and dark and a cold night wind made the shadows of the trees dance like grim spirits in the moonlight. Snakes, and spiders, and things too icky to mention slithered and scuttled among the rotting leaves and muck on the forest floor. It was exactly the sort of place ogres love best, and it wasn't long before Sir Fartsalot thought he spied one ahead.

He motioned for the others to halt and pointed to a tree with flaps of rough burlap clothing bulging out from behind it on either side. It was an ogre, all right. And a fat one by the look of it. Hiding behind a tree that wasn't half big enough to conceal him.

"Well," said Sir Cedric, "looks like the princesses weren't fibbing after all."

The ogre saw that he was discovered and bolted off through the trees with a scuttling, shambling, hunched-over ogre's gait.

Sir Fartsalot and Sir Cedric gave chase. Fealty and Sir Cedric's horse Codswallop picked their way expertly between the trees, and Harry spurred Wildfire to keep up with them. He certainly didn't want to fall behind now that he knew the forest was full of ogres.

The ogre led them over a muddy brook and through a nasty thorn patch and nearly lost them among some low-hanging trees, which the knights had to hack aside with sweeping swordswipes.

But finally they cornered the brute in a small clearing.

Harry had never laid eyes on any ogres before. In fact, he'd always thought they were a mere plot gimmick invented by traveling taletellers. This one was squat and hairy, with huge hands and even huger, leathery ears. Harry couldn't see his face because the ogre was trembling against a tree, covering his eyes in his hands and making scared, sniffling noises.

"Stop that blubbering!" Sir Cedric commanded. "Turn and face your doom at the hands of Sir Fartsalot the Brave, Sir Cedric the Thick, and Prince Harry the Tougher Than

He Looks." He gave Harry a wink. "As noble a quintuplet of knights as ever swung the sword!" Sir Cedric added.

"Wot?" the ogre asked. He peeked out from behind his hands with one eye. Immediately, he ceased trembling and straightened up. "Och, it's only a coupla knights!" he said, sounding relieved.

"Hey fellas," he called. "Come on out! It's only a coupla knights."

Suddenly ogres stepped out from behind every tree. There were dozens of them, ogres of all smells and sizes, the biggest standing taller than Sir Cedric atop Codswallop. And every one of them was armed—with clubs, or axes, or chains, or pointed sticks, or boards with nails poking out, or wet towels to wind and snap. They had Harry and the knights surrounded.

"Phew!" one of the ogres said. "We thought you was princesses."

Harry and the knights were hopelessly outnumbered. But still the ogres hung back, afraid to get too close to the knights' swords.

Finally, one of the boldest ogres advanced toward them, thrusting a spearpoint ahead of him.

"Come one step nearer, you vile unmentionable," Sir Fartsalot warned, "and I shall brast your pate!"

"You'll what?"
the ogre scoffed,
coming closer.

Sir Fartsalot
whanged him in the head
with Lucille.

"Oh," said the ogre.
"*Riiiiiiight*..."

He plunked over on
his face, out cold.

Then, with a terrifying din of howls, and whoops, and pounding war drums, and fingernails dragged across little chalk slates, all the ogres rushed them at once. The battle was on!

Sir Fartsalot flailed left and right with his trusty Lucille, while Sir Cedric hewed ogres like he was swatting flies. In one nifty piece of sword work, he felled three in a single swipe, then brained another quite by accident on his backswing.

Even the horses pitched in, butting, biting, kicking and trampling. Wildfire was overenjoying himself so vigorously that ogres scattered from his path in terror.

But at last, while the horse was administering a particularly brutal wedgie to an unlucky foe, one of the bravest and sneakiest ogres tiptoed up and grabbed hold of Harry's leg.

Harry yelled and tried to kick the fiend away. But the ogre held tight, trying to sink his teeth into the prince's ankle.

Harry lashed out in terror— and the ogre fell back, clutching a gash on his arm. Without thinking, Harry had drawn his sword and scored a hit!

"Well done, Harry!" Sir Fartsalot complimented. He had dismounted and was hacking his way through a throng of the spear-wielding brutes. But even as he spoke, an ogre grabbed him about the head, while another got hold of his sword arm. Two more wrapped themselves around his legs. A fifth got down on all fours behind him. Another four rushed at him using a log for a battering ram . . .

The log struck Sir Fartsalot square in the chest and knocked him flying backwards. In an instant, the brave old knight was buried under a swarm of pounding, punching, poking, pinching ogres.

"Sir Farts—" Harry started to call out. But before he could finish, he too was overpowered and dragged from his saddle.

16

Close up, the ogre was horrible-looking, and even more—far, far more—horrible-smelling. His skin was leathery and moistly lumpy, like the skin of a ham. He reeked of dirty socks steeped in swamp water that skunks had bathed in. He wore an apron and held a large wooden spoon. Reaching out two filthy fingers, he pinched Harry's cheek.

"Mmm ... tender," the ogre said discriminatingly.

Harry was bound to a stake, with sticks and logs piled about his feet. Beside him, Sir Fartsalot and Sir Cedric were tied up in huge iron pots simmering over two campfires. It was the next day, and sun shone down through the trees.

"Roast prince and knights boiled in the shell," the ogre said, smacking his lips. "Finest feast we've 'ad round 'ere in ages."

He added spices to the bubbling pots.

"Hey, easy there!" growled Sir Cedric. "Don't oversalt me!"

The ogre grinned a wicked, epicurean grin and sat down to peel and chop vegetables: bloodroot, skunk cabbage, poison ivy, nettles, thorns, dandelion roots, toadstools, and (shudder) *broccoli*.

"You slimy crouton!" Sir Cedric spat. "I hope I don't agree with you!"

You had to hand it to these knights, Harry thought. They never lost their fighting spirit. And all around the camp were ogres with black eyes, heads wrapped in bandages, and arms in slings to prove it.

"Let this be a lesson to you, Prince Harry," Sir Cedric added in a more reflective tone. "This is what comes of helping princesses."

The ogre sprang up in fright. He clasped his hands over his ears, dropping a paring knife to the ground. A milkweed he was peeling rolled into the fire.

"Don't speak that word!" the ogre yelped.

"What word?" Sir Cedric said. "'Princesses?'"

"Aaeeiiaaa!!!" the ogre shrieked, as if stuck by a pin. "I told you not to say that!

"Oh, how they plague us!" he groaned, hunching and cowering. "Nowhere in the forest is we safe. We keeps to the damp dark places and creeps about only at night, so as to avoid 'em. But they *still* won't leave us be." The ogre shuddered. Then, still a bit jumpy, he squatted and went on peeling vegetables.

"Well, now I've seen everything," Sir Cedric said. "Ogres afraid of princesses." (The ogre jumped and dropped another milkweed into the fire with a curse.) "Well, Sir Fartsalot, old friend, how are you doing?"

"I'm coming along nicely, thank you," the old knight replied. "Nice gentle simmer. It's a slow and painful way to die, but at least it'll bring out my flavors. And you, Sir Cedric?"

"Oh, I'm ruined!" Sir Cedric complained. "Saltier than sardines! It's not the way I wanted to go out, I don't mind telling you. But never mind me. How's the prince?"

"I'm all right," Harry said, trying to match the knights' bravery. "At least they haven't lit me on fire yet."

"That's the spirit, Your Majesty," Sir Cedric said. "Every cloud has a silver anniversary, as I always say. And don't worry, we'll have you out of there soon enough." There was a pause, and Sir Cedric grew thoughtful. "Somehow..." he added, at length.

"Yes," Sir Fartsalot agreed. "Somehow..."

And they both fell silent.

**17**

But time passed, and when at last the ogre chef was ready to light the pile of kindling at Harry's feet, the two knights still had not puzzled a way out.

"Don't worry now, Yer 'ighness," the ogre said, choosing a flaming branch from the fire under Sir Fartsalot. "You won't feel a thing—apart from the unbearable searing pain, that is. *Heh heh heh.*

"Oh, you might want to scream a little," the ogre added as an afterthought. "It won't do you no good, of course. But we ogres like to 'ear our entrees suffer."

"Harm a hair on that boy's head," Sir Fartsalot warned, "and I shall dispatch you straight to Heck!"

"Oh, yeah? You and wot army?" the ogre scoffed, and gave the old knight a stir with his spoon.

"Why, I'll—" Sir Cedric began, but he trailed off, unable to think of any threat he was in a position to make good on. "I hope you choke on me!" was the best he could come up with.

The ogre set flame to a tiny twig at the end of one of the skinniest sticks at Harry's feet. The prince held his breath as he watched it catch, then burn out, then catch again. The ogre chuckled. He was toying with Harry, drawing out his terror for his own amusement.

"Well, Sir Cedric, it would seem that here ends our final crusade," Sir Fartsalot eulogized. "My only regret is that I failed the prince."

"And mine, Sir Fartsalot," Sir Cedric replied. "Adieu, old friend."

Then, a bloodcurdling scream split the air.

"Oooooooooooooooooooo!"

An icy chill passed through the hearts of ogre and knight alike.

The ogre chef scrambled about in panic.

"No ... no ..." he trembled. "It c-c-can't be!"

"Ooooooo, Sir Fartsalot!" the voice repeated. "You look so *dashing* in that pot!"

That's right, it was one of the princesses.

Suddenly, all was a blizzard of taffeta and lace and twinkling tiaras, as an ambush of princesses descended on the ogre camp! Gowns flapped in fury. High-heels kicked viciously. Fists flew in a flash of sparkling rings.

In truth, the ogres put up little fight. The poor creatures were paralyzed with terror from the moment the first embroidered bodice appeared. Within minutes, the rout was complete, and there was nothing left for the pugilistic princesses to do but make sport of the vanquished by pulling off their hats, and yanking their tender ears, and lashing them to trees with their own skipping ropes.

But they soon abandoned these warlike pursuits to fall all over one another rescuing Sir Fartsalot and Sir Cedric. They untied the knights and helped them out from the iron pots. Then they pushed and shoved for a chance to mop the knights' faces with their veils.

Gwendolyn and Daisy appeared. The dragon patted

out the fire around Harry's ankles with its tail while Gwendolyn untied him.

"Captured by mere ogres," Gwendolyn said, shaking her head. "You princes can be so helpless sometimes."

Her sisters had made up their minds that it would be terribly romantic for Sir Fartsalot and Sir Cedric to return with them to the castle. There, the princesses would minister to their wounds and nurse them back to strength, and naturally the brave knights would fall in love with their angels of mercy. But there were so many competing claims for each patient's heart that the angels of mercy soon fell to arguing and making unladylike remarks.

And while the princesses quarreled, the knights snuck away to where their horses were tied and made another narrow escape.

Harry said goodbye to Gwendolyn, and he and Wildfire soon caught up with the two knights on the trail. They were slumped listlessly in their saddles, looking broken and soggy—not from simmering for several hours at low heat so much as with the shame of being rescued from death's jaws by a bunch of princesses.

"Let us never speak of it," Sir Fartsalot urged solemnly.

"Speak of what?" replied Sir Cedric, signifying he understood.

S o, Harry and the two knights resumed their journey through Knockon Wood without any mention of ogres or princesses. That is, except for something Sir Fartsalot happened to bring up on the trail the next morning.

"I say, Sir Cedric," the old knight said, his mood lifted somewhat by a hearty breakfast of turnips benedict. "Did you happen to catch that nifty piece of swordwork by young Harry here yesterday?"

"You mean when that rat tried to grab his ankle?" Sir Cedric replied. "I certainly did. Ho, ho! The dirty sneak will feel that a while!"

• • •

Later that day, at a place marked by a dead and hollow oak, they came upon a fortune-teller's tent.

"Aah, a soothsayer," Sir Fartsalot said. "Perhaps she can advise us in our quest."

"Actually, Sir Farty," Sir Cedric said, "I'd been meaning to have a word with you about this so-called 'Booger' you're after ..."

Harry felt a surge of panic. As much as he hated to see Sir Fartsalot embarrass himself, he wasn't ready for him to find out their whole quest was a hoax, either.

But Sir Fartsalot replied, "You're right, Sir Cedric. This soothsayer *could* help us find the Booger faster."

Sir Cedric rolled his eyes but said nothing. Harry was off the hook, at least for the moment.

There was nobody in sight, so they got down from their horses and went to the tent's entrance.

"Hello?" Sir Fartsalot called. "Anybody in there?"

"Enter…" answered a voice from within that sounded strangely thin and distant.

So Sir Fartsalot pulled the tent flap back and they stepped through…

Inside, the tent was dark as midnight, and thick wisps of fog swirled around them. . . . Ahead was a dim light. . . . They walked and walked toward it through the fog. Harry was just thinking it was impossible they could have taken so many steps in the tiny tent when suddenly the mists parted and they came upon a gypsy woman seated behind a small table.

MADAME FLADNAR

FORTUNES READ, YOUR DEATH FORETOLD WHILE U WAIT

She wore a rainbow-colored turban and a veil that hid most of her face. A candle flickered at one corner of the table.

The gypsy woman did not look up as they approached. She was busy playing solitaire with a deck of tarot cards.

"Are you Madame Fladnar?" Sir Fartsalot asked.

"Oo, a psychic," she said. Her voice was rather husky for a woman. "You must be part geepsy."

"No, we're knights," Sir Fartsalot said. "We hoped you might help us in a grave and urgent quest."

"I knew zat, of course," she scoffed.

She brought out a crystal ball with a slot at the top like a piggy bank and set it on the table in front of her. She took a deep breath, closed her eyes, and pressed her fingers to her temples...

After a moment, she spoke in a trancelike voice... "Please..." she intoned.

Sir Fartsalot hung on her words.

"...insert..."

He leaned closer. He didn't want to miss a word of her prophecy.

"...coin."

Madame Fladnar opened her eyes and winked at them over her veil.

"Takes a little 'prophet incentive' to get it vorking," she explained.

Sir Fartsalot took out a small money purse and tipped three gold pieces into his hand. He dropped one in the slot.

There was a clink, and instantly the crystal ball filled with swirling wisps of blue, and red, and green, and off-green mist. Madame Fladnar peered into the ball.

"I see zat you have journeyed many miles…"

Sir Fartsalot nudged Sir Cedric, who looked unimpressed.

"Seeking a terrible creature …" Madame Fladnar continued.

"Lucky guess," Sir Cedric muttered under his breath.

"A creature so horribly vicked …" Madame Fladnar said, looking Sir Cedric in the eye, "zat people fear even to speak eets name…"

Sir Cedric started in surprise. Sir Fartsalot grew giddy with expectation. Both knights gawked at the crystal ball.

So they didn't notice when Madame Fladnar's veil slipped out of place. She quickly refastened it, but not before Harry caught a glimpse of moustache.

Where had he seen that moustache before?

"For many months now, you have followed a mizzterious omen," she went on.

"The Foul West Wind!" Sir Fartsalot agreed.

"Ah, zat is vhat you *szink*," Madame Fladnar said.

> *"I see zat you are brave of arm and true*
> *of heart,*
>
> *And all you vant is to do your part;*
>
> *But I'm afraid to say zat from zee start,*
>
> *Zis force driving you onward was actually*
> *just a—"*

Harry's eyes widened. Sir Cedric's jaw dropped.

> *"—manifeztation of your strong sense of*
> *public duty."*

"I see," Sir Fartsalot said, though in fact he looked rather puzzled. "But tell us, how shall we find the beast we seek?"

Madame Fladnar stared into the crystal ball. She frowned.

"Aah, zat I cannot say..." she said, mysteriously.

"Why not?" Sir Fartsalot asked.

"Because I'm afraid your time eez up. You vill have to insert anozzer coin."

Sir Fartsalot dropped another gold piece in the slot, and the ball began to glow and cloud up again.

Madame Fladnar stared into the crystal ball.

"I see a road zat ends at zee beginning..." she went on. "And many dangers ahead . . . I see an untimely parting...And a timely reunion...Or two...You vill meet an unexpected traveler...And zhen...Oh, my..."

"What?" begged Sir Fartsalot. "Go on..."

"Sorry," she said. "Time'z up again."

Sir Fartsalot hastily put his last coin in the slot. The gypsy woman peered into the crystal ball and continued:

"I see a great battle..."

"Yes?"

"Ending in a glorious victory..."

"Aha!" Sir Fartsalot clapped his hands together in delight. "Most excellent!"

"…For eizher you or your adversary."

"Oh."

Then suddenly a dark look came over Madame Fladnar. Her eyes widened in horror.

"What is it?" begged Sir Fartsalot. "What do you see?"

"I see…Nope, sorry," Madame Fladnar said. "You vill need anozzer gold piece."

"But I haven't any!" Sir Fartsalot said. "That was my last!"

Madame Fladnar shrugged.

"Please!" Sir Fartsalot begged. "This is a matter of great public urgency!"

"Sir Knight, I vill give you zis piece of advice," Madame Fladnar said. "Believe in your qvuest, alzhough only a fool would. For zherein lies your only hope.

"You know," she added in a slightly different voice, "people often underestimate the wisdom of Fools."

As she said this, she gave Harry a wink—and suddenly he remembered where he'd seen her moustache before.

"Your words," Sir Fartsalot said, "are they a riddle that holds some clue to help us in our quest?"

"Nope," the fortune-teller replied. "Just something my dear old mammy used to say."

Sir Fartsalot looked perplexed.

"Madam," he said, narrowing his eyes in suspicion, "are you *really* a gypsy seer?"

"Of course," she replied. "Vhy else vould I speak vith zis silly accent?"

She put the crystal ball away under the table. Then she picked up her deck of tarot cards and continued her game of solitaire, taking no further notice of them.

"Let's go, Sir Farty," Sir Cedric said, putting a hand on his friend's shoulder. "We don't need a crystal ball to tell us when we've been had."

They took two steps backward and suddenly found themselves outside the tent again, squinting in bright sunlight. There was nothing for them to do but get back on their horses and head onward.

19

The road from the gypsy's tent wound deeper and deeper into the forest. They turned left, then left, then left, then left, until finally they came to a place marked by a hollow oak tree. Here the path split off in two directions. A wooden sign marking the first road warned:

ENCHANTED FOREST:

BEWARE OF BUGABOOS, MUMBO JUMBOS

AND THINGS THAT ONLY EXIST IN YOUR IMAGINATION

An arrow pointing the other way read:

DETOUR:

LONG WAY ROUND

"Oh, man!" Harry exclaimed. "An Enchanted Forest!"

As much as Harry always loved magic, he'd only ever seen the parlor trick variety of stage magicians. He'd never encountered any real magic, such as wizards and enchanters used. Now here he was, on the brink of a bonafide Enchanted Forest! It was the most exciting moment of the entire quest.

But to his surprise, the knights halted at the cross-roads. Usually so quick to throw themselves in the path of danger, they refused to set foot in the magical wood.

"Dragons and ogres are one thing," Sir Cedric frowned. "But we don't want to get mixed up with a lot of magic if we can help it."

"But I thought we knights craved adventure?" Harry asked (for indeed he had begun to think of himself as a knight).

"Magic is a tricky foe, Harry," Sir Fartsalot explained. "One that can't be trusted. One moment you can be battling a mighty monster, then suddenly—*poof!*—the monster transforms into a chickadee."

"Or from a chickadee to a mighty monster," added Sir Cedric. "It's enough to drive a fighting man batty."

"Can't we at least have a look around?" Harry pleaded.

But the knights merely covered their ears against his pleas and started off down the detour route, eager to put the Enchanted Forest as far behind them as possible.

. . .

It was well into evening when they finally stopped to make camp for the night. After dinner, sitting around the fire sipping turnip cider, Sir Fartsalot began to wax philosophical.

"I tell you, Sir Cedric," he said waxily. "I feel my questing days are nearing their end."

"Maybe you shouldn't sit around the fire like that," Sir Cedric warned. Sir Fartsalot had had a few ciders, and Sir Cedric was worried the old knight might go up like a Roman candle if a spark caught him.

"No, Sir Cedric, don't try to change my mind," Sir Fartsalot replied. "Once noble Harry and I have slain the dreaded Booger and restored safety to the realm, I shall hang up my sword and retire to a quieter life."

Hearing this, Harry nearly choked on his turnip pudding (which he had been gagging on anyway).

"After all, this is my worthiest quest in a long career of public service," Sir Fartsalot waxed on. "Let it be what I am remembered by."

Harry couldn't meet Sir Fartsalot's eyes. He turned quickly away—only to find Sir Cedric glaring a glare at him that would scour iron.

A strange feeling sprang up inside Harry then. One that had been gnawing at him for days. Harry didn't know what this queer new feeling was. He thought maybe it was gas.

But it wasn't. It was his conscience.

For Harry had grown to love Sir Fartsalot. Yes, even to respect him. For the old knight was as brave and true as his reputation. So it made Harry sick now to think of phonies like Sir Bedwetter laughing at him behind his back.

*Oh, how could people be so rotten?* he asked himself.

20

The next morning, Harry rose before the others and strolled off down the path they had traveled the night before. He wanted to be alone, to think.

He knew he had to find some way to put Sir Fartsalot off his quest. But how, without admitting the Booger was a hoax?

Harry turned the problem over and over in his mind, tossing it from his on-the-one-hand to his on-the-other-hand. But in the end he knew from the start what he had to do all along...

Lie.

Make something up.

Cover his butt.

His heart told him it was the right thing to do.

Caught up in his thoughts, Harry lost track of how far he had wandered down the path. Still, he was amazed when he found himself back at the entrance to the Enchanted Forest, for it seemed to him this point should've been hours behind them on the trail.

Yet there, unmistakably, was the sign: "Enchanted Forest: Beware of Bugaboos, Mumbo Jumbos, and Figments of Your Imagination."

*What could it hurt?* Harry thought. *Probably the old knights were just being superstitious.*

"I wouldn't if I was you."

Harry whirled around. He looked up, and down, and sideways. Then he looked up, and down, and sideways again. But there was nothing to see but an owl on a branch.

Harry squinted at the owl. "Did you say that?" he asked, skeptically.

"Oh, no. Not *I*," the owl replied. Its voice was full of sarcasm and wounded dignity. "You must be imagining things."

The owl had strange markings about its eyes and beak that almost resembled spectacles and a moustache.

"Wow, talking birds!" Harry exclaimed.

"Bird, singular," the owl corrected him. "And there's nothing special as far as that goes. All creatures possess the power of speech, naturally. It's you humans who are usually too dull to understand. Really, though, enter this wood and you'll be sorry. It's full of Bugaboos and Mumbo Jumbos and..."

"'Things That Only Exist In Your Imagination,'" Harry finished. "So I've heard. But can you blame me if I want to take a look for myself?"

"Oh, you shall get more than a look, I'll bet," the owl said, more to itself than to Harry. "Indeed you shall."

But the owl itself was so incredible, if a bit of a nag, that Harry was only more curious to see what other wonders the forest might hold.

So he tiptoed a little ways in. He told himself he would turn back at the first hint of trouble. And he would be careful not to stray from the path, for he knew from stories that was how most of the trouble in Enchanted Forests started...

But there was magic in the very air, a tingle of possibility, drawing Harry forward as if in a trance...

He had hardly rounded the first bend in the path when a blinking cloud of fireflies appeared ahead of him, arranging and rearranging themselves into words, like flashing signs:

"MAGICAL" they blinked..."MARVELS" [*blink*] ... "AHEAD!"...

"BE-"..."HOLD"...

"BE-"..."DAZZLING"...

"BE-"..."SPECTACLES!"...

Soon he came to a place where the path was lined by the most fantastic flowers, in rainbow-colored stripes and paisleys and polka dots. Harry went closer to pick a few—

But suddenly all the flower tops rose into the air!

Transformed into butterflies! They fluttered away in a mass, leaving bare, green stems behind.

Then, just ahead, three frogs in tiny waistcoats crossed the path, leapfrogging over each other's shoulders.

Harry drifted on in a daze of wild wonder as the path wound and wended deeper into the wemarkable wood.

He was startled back to his senses when he tripped over a tree root and scraped his knee. While he picked himself up, the leaves of the trees around him shook as if in a sudden breeze.

But there was no breeze ...

Something about that made Harry nervous. It suddenly occurred to him how far he had wandered into the forest. He turned to go back ...

But his way was blocked by a wall of trees! The path had disappeared!

Harry hesitated ... He didn't want to get lost deeper in the forest ... But there was no way back ...

So he went on.

The path seemed to be shifting ahead of Harry, as if steering him somewhere. And whenever he turned to look back it had vanished behind him ...

Finally the trail brought him to a sunlit glade with a brook running through it.

The water was too wide and swift to cross. So there was nothing for Harry to do but sit here and rest.

And, oh, what a peaceful spot it was! Soft music rose from the brook, like notes played on the flute. And to its tune, dragonflies and bees swirled to and fro in dancing pairs. Along the bank, flowers whirled like pinwheels in the breeze.

Harry should have been on his guard, for he knew that in stories such magical places often had a dangerous, drowsying effect. But he was up soooooo early, and he had walked soooooo (*yawn*) long, and oh (*stretch*), it felt sooooo good just to ...

## 21

**H**arry was jolted back to his senses by a terrifying roar. It was like nothing he had ever heard before, yet strangely familiar...

**"Garble$#%bargle!&^gargle*#$bagel!!!"**

Something massive was crashing through the trees on the other side of the brook. And it was coming this way! Frantically, Harry looked about for a place to hide.

"Psst! Over here!"

It was the owl, beckoning him from behind a large rock. Harry scrambled over and took cover just in time. For crashing out of the woods on the far bank came an enormous monster!

It was huge and hideously deformed, like something from a dimly recalled nightmare. It had several arms jutting out at odd angles, a huge misshapen mouth of jagged teeth, and a nose where its ear should have been. And spattered all over its shaggy mass were eyes that pointed off in all directions at once. It looked like a puzzle that had been put together all wrong.

The monster paused by the brook's edge.

Harry scrunched down, frozen with terror.

"W-what is *that*?" he whispered. He peeked over the boulder again. The monster was picking its teeth with a spruce tree.

"It hasn't got a name," replied the owl. "In fact, I doubt there ever was such a thing. You've probably just imagined it."

"You m-mean it's not r-real?" Harry stuttered.

He looked over the rock again. The beast was grinding boulders into piles of dust to amuse itself.

"Oh, it's *real*, all right," the owl said. "But only because you've imagined it."

Harry was puzzled.

"Remember where you are, my boy," the owl said.

Then Harry recalled the warning: "The Enchanted Forest: Full of Things That Only Exist In Your Imagination . . ."

The next moment, the monster roared a pitiless roar—and Harry knew it had discovered him.

Sure enough, the beast crossed the brook in one hop and lumbered toward him, walking on its knuckles like an ape.

22

"**Y**ikes!" Harry squeaked. "Help! W-where can I run?" "I'd say you're cornered," the owl remarked matter-of-factly. "You'd never out-run it anyway."

The beast thumped toward them.

"Please!" Harry begged, in a tiny voice. "Help me!"

"There's nothing *I* can do, I'm afraid," the owl said, taking flight. "You're the one who imagined the ghastly thing..."

The owl flapped up beyond the monster's reach.

The ferocious nightmare loomed right over Harry. It snatched him up and held him to its armpit for a closer look.

"So," the owl called down, "I expect it's up to you to *un*imagine it."

"*Un*imagine it?" said Harry. "W-what do you mean?"

"Clear it from your mind entirely!" the owl shouted. "Think of something else!"

Harry understood. But it was far easier said than done. For the creature's grip was crushing his sides. And Harry was looking straight into its enormous mouth, over spiky banks of teeth and down its cavernous throat. And worst of all was the reek from the beast's armpit, which would've brought tears to the eyes of a troll.

"*#Rumble*&%rumpus*@bungle*&&%fungus*!!!"

Harry squeezed his eyes shut and plugged his nose. He tried desperately to block the creature out of his mind. He forced himself to imagine something pleasant . . .

The cozy warmth of his bed in the castle when he had slept in late . . .

"Ug*&%drub*@gob*&%wampum#@*twee?$!!!"

His only memory of his mother, bending over him in a halo of light . . .

"#%$Schmarffle@*$*barffle#$@*I#*feel%&*arffle . . ."

Cuddly newborn kittens . . .

"$*Eenie&#%$meanie*&%$miney&@#%mmmrrrr ooowwww . . ."

Harry landed hard on his rump. The pain in his sides

had suddenly disappeared, and with it the horrible smell. He opened his eyes...

"Mrrrooowww."

The monster was gone. In its place was a tiny grey kitten.

The kitten brushed against his legs. Harry bent forward to pet it.

Then he remembered the owl.

"Hey, thanks," he said, looking around. But the owl was gone. "Wait!" he called out. "How do I get out of—"

Something fell over Harry's head and everything went dark. A loop tightened about his feet, and he was tripped to the ground.

"I got him!" boomed a pair of voices that were like the echo in a bell tower.

**23**

"**Y**ou got him?!" said one of the voices. "You mean *I* did." "What? Oh, that is so like you," said the other voice. "Just sit back and let me do all the work, then try to hog the credit."

Harry found himself trapped in a cramped, pitch-dark sack. He squirmed and struggled against its sides. He groped around until he found the mouth of the sack, then yanked at it with all his might. But it wouldn't budge.

"Hah! *That's* a good one!" one of the voices went on. "*You* couldn't catch a cold without me. Face it, you're all left feet."

"Oh, *please*! I've been carrying you on my shoulders for years. You've never done anything without me."

The voices boomed high above, like echoes in a

mountain pass. *Giants*, Harry thought with sinking heart. *Two of them*.

Finally the giants dropped their argument, but promptly struck up another over which one of them would have to carry their catch. When at last *that* was settled, Harry was hoisted off the ground and borne away. It was a bumpy ride, bouncing along over a giant's shoulder, and Harry could make out only snatches of the pair's conversation. But he heard enough to wish he hadn't:

"He'll be fabulous in a cream sauce."

"No, no. There's not enough of him. I say we serve him in a salad."

After a while, Harry felt himself being lifted straight up, then up, then up again, as if mounting the steps of some endless ladder.

Finally he was plopped down on what felt like a hard wooden floor. Harry soon gathered they were in the giants' dwelling.

"Tea?" asked one of the giants.

"I'd love a cup," said the other giant.

"Make me one too, then, will you?" said the other giant.

"Hmph!" humphed the other giant. "You've got some nerve!"

But a moment later Harry heard the clatter of stove-wood, the snick of a match being struck, and the hiss of a wet kettle put over a flame.

"Now," said one of the voices, "let's have a look at our catch."

The drawstring of the sack was loosened and Harry was tipped out onto the floor.

He found himself in a one-room hut. It was an ordinary room, full of homey comforts—a straw bed with embroidered pillows, some half-finished knitting resting on a rocking chair, a blood-smeared club standing by the hearth. But everything was gigantic in scale, as if seen from a mouse's eye view.

Harry did not take in all of this at once, mind you, for he was struck with amazement by his first look at his captors . . . Or captor . . . Or, that is . . .

You see, standing over Harry was the hulking form of a mighty giant, as tall as an oak, with two legs like great tree trunks, and two arms like stone columns—and set upon its massive shoulders, not one but two giant heads, on two giant necks.

For they (or it) were (or was) a two-headed giant. Or two one-bodied giants. Or Siamese-twin giants.

But whatever you called it (e.g., "them"), the massive body bent over Harry, and both heads examined him with a scrutiny he did not at all like.

"Mmmmm," said the right head. "He looks like a yummy morsel."

"A tasty tidbit," agreed the left head. "Not very filling, though."

"True. More of a snack-sized portion."

"Oh, but where are your manners?" scolded the head on the left. "Offer our guest some refreshment."

The right head made a face at the left, but smiled politely to Harry and said, "Can I get you some tea and cake?"

Harry was much too terrified to have any appetite. And he wasn't too sure about the cooking of giants (he recalled hearing something about them "grinding bones to make their bread"). But rather than risk offending them, he said, "Th-thank you. That would be, uh, n-nice."

"You see, the poor thing's starving!" said the head on the left. "Well, what are you waiting for? Hurry up and get him some fruitcake!"

"Hurry up yourself, you lazy hippo!"

And so, grumbling and griping, the two-headed giant bustled over to the other side of the hut, where Harry saw (gulp!) an enormous cookstove. The giants lifted a teapot as big as an inn and brought it to the table.

Then the giants slipped on an apron and flitted about the hut, dusting countertops and corners with one hand while the other hand swept the floors using a broom made out of a willow tree.

"Forgive the mess," the head on the left apologized.

"We weren't expecting company," explained the right.

Finally they finished tidying. Then they lifted Harry over to the table and gently set him down on one of the chairs. He was so high, it made his head spin to look down. But the table's edge still loomed far above him.

"Really, where's your head?" said the giant on the left. "Get him some cushions!"

The giants bustled away and came back plumping two enormous pillows to set under Harry.

They broke him off a crumb of fruitcake that would have fed ten burly knights for a week.

"Well, this is nice," said the head on the left. "We don't get many visitors."

"I'm Blog," said the head on the right. Then, behind his hand, he added, "The good-looking one."

"And I'm Grog," said the head on the left, then whispered so the other wouldn't hear, "The handsome one."

To Harry, the two heads looked identical. And as gruesome as any ogre or princess he had met in his adventures so far.

"M-my name's Harry," he squeaked.

"Harry?!" Blog snorted. "What a funny name!"

Grog's mouth fell open.

"Really, you have the manners of a troll," he said in disgust. "Ignore him, Harry. You have a lovely name. Welcome to our humble home. It's no castle—"

"But the location is good," Blog added.

Harry wondered what Blog meant by that. From where he was sitting, he could see nothing outside the hut's windows but blank blue sky, unbroken by tree or hill or anything else that might have given him some clue where he was.

That might have puzzled Harry, but his mind was on other matters. While the giants went on making small talk, he snuck glances around the hut, looking for some way of escape. The windows were miles too high, with nothing nearby he might scramble up. And as for the hut's massive oaken door, it would take an army of men to open it. But along the base of the door there was a spot where light spilled in through a crack.

Might it be big enough for him to squeeze through?

21

"You've hardly touched your fruitcake," Grog said with concern. "Don't you like it?" "He baked it," Blog whispered, making a face.

"Look, Harry, if you're worried about certain *rumors* . . ." Grog said, "all that business about 'the blood of Englishmen'...It simply isn't true."

"Some of it's true," Blog said.

"Well, okay, some of it's true," Grog conceded. "But I promise you, Harry, this fruitcake is one-hundred-percent-bone-dust-free."

"It's the raisins," Blog said. "I told you, nobody likes raisins."

"It's a *fruit*cake," Grog replied. "It's *supposed* to have raisins."

"No, it's fine," Harry said. "Really."

"Then what's the matter?" Grog asked. "Because something's bothering you, I can tell. It's written all over your face."

"Shouldn't keep things bottled up," Blog said. "Let it out. Get it off your chest. You'll feel better."

"Whatever it is," Grog prodded, "you can tell us. We're all friends now."

"Well . . . it's just that . . ." Harry hesitated. Then he decided he had nothing to lose. "Are you still going to eat me?"

"Eat you!" the giants gasped, horrified.

"Heavens, no!" Grog said.

"Do we look like a couple of cannibals to you?" Blog said.

Harry chose not to answer that.

"Ugh!" Grog said. "Why, the very idea makes me queasy!"

"We would never eat a pal, Harry," Blog said. "So don't worry about that."

Harry was relieved.

He sighed and ate a bit of his fruitcake. It wasn't bad actually. Though of course Blog was right about the raisins.

"No, no, no, we're not going to *eat* you," Blog said, laughing at the very idea.

"We're going to feed you to our pet," Grog added.

Harry choked on his fruitcake.

"Your *p-pet*?" he sputtered.

"Tweety," Blog explained. "She's a baby roc. You know, gigantic bird of myth and legend?"

"You'll love her!" said Grog. "She's adorable."

"So cute and fluffy."

"And very advanced for her age."

"She can polish off a cow in two gulps, bones and all!"

"But would you listen to us!" Grog blushed. "I hope you can excuse a mother's pride, Harry."

"Go on," Blog urged Grog, "tell him how we found her."

Then Grog told the story of how Tweety's mother had abandoned her in the nest when she was only an egg. Blog and Grog had found the tiny orphan among the highest crags at the peak of Mount Kaboom. They knew it would perish if left to the elements. So day and night, for more than a week, they sat upon the poor motherless egg themselves. Finally a crack formed in the egg's shell, then spread ... And the next moment, a small sharp beak poked through! Blog and Grog jumped straight into the air with excitement. (Also because the beak had jabbed them in the butt.)

Out popped the baby roc. She was only tiny then, hardly bigger than a full-grown ostrich. One glimpse of her melted the giants' hearts.

"There she was," Blog sighed. "A poor little hatchling, all alone in the world. Nobody to love. Nobody to eat."

Well, their maternal instincts got the best of them. They couldn't just abandon her, not again. So they named her Tweety, after an uncle of theirs, and nursed her on a bottle until she was old enough to start on solid food. Then they fed her first on rodents, small reptiles, and an occasional traveling poet. But as she grew and grew, so did her appetite.

"So you see," Grog said, wiping his eyes, "we've been like a mother to her."

"The mother she never had," Blog added, punctuating his remark with a sniffle.

Then both giants reached for their hanky and, finding there was only one, soon fell to quarrelling over it.

• • •

Harry had made up his mind. He was going to have to make a dash for that gap under the door the first opportunity he got and take his chances with whatever he found on the other side.

He waited all afternoon for his chance, but the giants never left him alone for one minute. They fussed over him like a doll, carrying him everywhere, tucking him in for a nap under a tea-cosy quilt in a baking-pan bed (which made him far too nervous to sleep a wink), and pouring tea into him until he made sloshing noises when he moved. They even insisted on burping him like a baby.

Harry thought he might wait until after the giants went to sleep. But then they started to get his bed ready for him in "Tweety's old room," a giant birdcage suspended from the ceiling. It was like some mid-air prison, with cage-wire as thick as iron bars. He saw there'd be no breaking out of *there*. And even if he did somehow manage to pick the lock or slip through a loose pair of bars, the drop to the floor would flatten him like one of Sir Fartsalot's turnip pancakes.

So he'd have to create some kind of diversion. And soon...

The giants had set him at the table for his sixth cup of tea and were over by the bedside laying out their pajamas for the night when Harry finally saw his chance.

"You know, I've never mentioned this before," Harry said, throwing his voice so it sounded like it was coming from over by the bed, "but you're ugly and you dress us funny."

"What?" Blog said.

"Excuse me?" Grog said.

"Hmph!" Blog humphed. "It's a little late for excuse-mes now!"

"I don't know what that's supposed to mean," Grog sniffed, "but what you said just now was uncalled for."

"What *I* said?" Blog retorted. "You're the one who started everything!"

But Grog wasn't listening. He had turned away in a huff. So Blog turned the other way in disgust. They gave each other the cold shoulder.

"And another thing," Harry added. "No offense, but you smell like a pig's armpit."

That was too much. The giants turned on each other and started arguing nose-to-nose.

"I never!" snorted Grog.

"Then maybe you should for once!" snapped Blog.

While they bickered, Harry shimmied to the edge of his cushion. But when he peered down at the floor so far below, he couldn't work up the courage to jump …

...until he thought of brave Sir Fartsalot and asked himself what the old knight would do.

Then before he could think twice, Harry had leapt from the chair-ledge and landed on all fours.

Unfortunately the force of his jump also tipped the chair backwards. It fell to the floor with a crash like mighty ships colliding. So much for his diversion.

"Oh, no!" Grog exclaimed. "The poor thing's fallen!"

"It's all your fault!" Blog said.

"*My* fault?" Grog replied. "You mustn't have set him properly in place, you oaf! Oh, dear!"

"Are you all right, Harry?"

The giants rushed over to pick Harry up. But he darted through their legs and raced for the crack in the door.

"Wait!" the giants called. "Be careful!"

But Harry didn't stop. In a flash he had reached the door. Sure enough, there was a hole along the threshold as big as an ordinary window...

Harry dove through—

And stopped dead when he reached the other side—

For he found himself looking *down* on cloudtops!

The giants' hut was mounted like a tree fort in the topmost branches of an impossibly tall beanstalk that stretched down, and down, and down, and down...

Harry was so high, whole vistas were reduced to the scale of toy battlefields. Directly below, the mighty forest of Knockon Wood looked like a clump of hedges. To the north, the craggy peaks of Mount Kaboom seemed scarcely more than an ambitious sand castle. And all around him stretched vast rolling mounds of clouds, like banks of white pillow-stuffing.

But those clouds would supply no soft landings, Harry knew. Too terrified to move, he clung to a leafstem as thick as an apple tree.

"Mind you don't slip," Grog warned, appearing in the doorway behind him. "It's a nasty fall."

"You'd be smashed to plup," Blog said. "You'd lose all your crunchiness."

"Why don't you come back in and finish your tea," Grog sniffed, as though Harry had offended his hospitality.

"We'll head off first thing tomorrow," Blog added, in the same curt tone. "Since you're in such a hurry."

## 25

S o they started out early the next morning, the giants climbing backwards down the endless beanstalk with Harry draped over Blog's shoulder. Harry's hands were tied with rope after his failed escape, but Blog and Grog had been careful not to make the knots too tight and kept asking after his comfort to an extent that was quite insufferable.

"How are you doing back there, Harry?" Blog asked.

"Not afraid of heights, I hope?" Grog said.

"Unghunghngrrr," Harry moaned in reply.

At last, mercifully, they struck ground and headed north. The giants traveled swiftly with their long strides, and the great peaks of Mount Kaboom loomed larger and ever larger ahead of them until soon they arrived at the base of a mighty cliff of sheer rock.

From high above came terrifying shrieks—birdlike, but of monstrous proportions:

**"CAW! CRRAW! CAWRRAW!"**

Harry heard them and all hope died. He knew whatever was behind that awful din must be a creature of purely mythical dimensions, full of bloodthirst and cruelty—and horribly, horribly tone-deaf.

"Mummy's coming, Tweety-pie," Grog called up.

Harry squirmed and struggled, realizing this was probably his last chance to escape.

"Help!" he screamed, kicking and thrashing. "Somebody! He-l-l-p-p!"

"Oh, stop," Grog chided. "You're making us feel awful."

Then, hand over hand, the giants started to climb the rocky precipice. Harry's stomach tightened as the world at ground level began to get small and far away again, then smaller and farther away.

At last, they gained the cliff.

The creature, when Harry saw it, was more monstrous than his worst imaginings. Bigger than the giants themselves, it had a beak like a guillotine and eyes that gleamed violent murder. The moment it saw them it began to beat its wings and claw its nest in fresh fury, shrieking its hunger and spite.

Suddenly, the birdbeast shot out its beak, snatched hold of one of the giants' legs and began dragging them toward its nest!

"Bad Tweety!" Grog scolded, clinging to a boulder. "We don't eat Mummy!"

"Naughty! You know better!" Blog said, but also added proudly, "Boy, feel the *power* in that beak of hers."

Still the birdbeast kept trying to yank them loose from their rockhold.

"Quick, try singing to her," Grog suggested, and both giants launched into a lullaby:

> *"We love you,*
> *You love we,*
> *We're a non-traditional*
> *Fam-i-ly…"*

But instead of letting go, the creature began to gnash its beak in chomping, chewing motions. Grog tried another tactic:

"Look," he said, dangling Harry. "Mummy brought you a treat…"

"Mmmm . . ." Blog coaxed. "Yummy, yummy…"

At last the feathered nightmare let go of their leg, and the giants stepped clear of its nest.

The beaked behemoth gnashed and screamed madly for its meat, but Grog was firm.

"Manners!" he scolded, holding Harry out of reach until the monster settled down. "Now, don't bolt your food, or you'll make yourself sick."

"Eat him a bit at a time," Blog urged. "He's not going anywhere."

And with that they tossed Harry to his doom in the birdbeast's nest.

160

## 26

The nest was a grisly clutter of bones and skulls and gory remains. The huge bird monster loomed over Harry, its eyes gleaming with bloodthirst ...

The mighty beak stretched forward to snatch him up, but Harry rolled out of the way and scrambled to his feet.

His wrists were still bound together, but it was the simplest of all magicians' tricks for him to slip them free. Then he picked a bone up off the nest's floor to use as a weapon. He swung it as hard as he could, knocking the deadly beak aside. But the monster just let out an angry, ear-splitting shriek and came at him once more.

The creature pecked at him savagely. But again and again, Harry batted its mighty beak aside and dodged out of reach.

But soon the monster had him backed up against the

side of the nest by the cliff's edge. Behind Harry was a sheer drop to the ground. There was no escape.

The monster lunged—and this time grabbed the bone in its terrible beak. Harry was lifted right off his feet as the birdbeast wrenched it from his hands. Then the monster slowly crunched up his feeble weapon and swallowed it, just for spite.

Harry crouched against the wall of the nest. With nowhere to hide and no way to defend himself, all he could do now was hope for a quick end...

The monster's shrill rage grew even more furious and off-key, until Harry thought he would faint from fear...

But for some reason the creature seemed to be looking past him. As if it had forgotten him momentarily...

The birdbeast squawked and carried on like mad. But its attention was focused on something far away among the clouds.

The giants too were peering off into the distance.

"I don't believe it!" said Blog.

"How dare she!" said Grog.

Far off, a huge pair of wings veered toward them, skimming the clouds.

"The nerve! Waltzing back in here now, after all this time."

With the sun directly behind it, Harry could make out only a silhouette. Like the shadow of some mighty bird. Or maybe a dragon?

"It just isn't fair!" Grog whined. "We've been more of a mother to her than that fly-by-night magpie ever was."

"Well, *I* won't let her steal our Tweety away now!" Blog said. "Over my dead body!"

"Mine too!" said Grog.

Harry watched as it drew closer. It didn't look like any bird he had ever seen. It was oddly stiff, and its edges glinted like steel in the sun.

Then suddenly it was upon them. It swooped up, casting a huge winged shadow over them, then nose-dived onto the cliff.

"Flee while you can, foul fiends of Heck!" cried a voice. "Or taste the wrath of Lucille!"

"I think I'm going to be sick . . ." added another voice behind that one.

It was Sir Fartsalot! And Sir Cedric!

What had landed on the cliff was no bird or dragon, but some fantastic winged contraption of leather and steel!

"Wow!" Harry gaped. "What kind of awesome magic is that?!"

"Not magic at all," Sir Fartsalot said. "Merely an invention of this remarkable tinkerer we met on the road. Fellow called it a 'hang glider.' How was that for a ride, eh, Sir Cedric?"

But Sir Cedric was bent over the edge of the cliff. Loud retching noises were his only reply.

"Phew!" Blog said, relieved. "It's only a pair of yeomen!"

"Oh, goody!" Grog added. "They'll make a splendid feast for Tweety!"

"Quit your yabbering!" Sir Cedric demanded, wiping his mouth with the back of his swordhand and rejoining the fray. "Arm yourselves and fight, you overstuffed, yellow-livered, incontinent chickens!"

At this, Tweety erupted in a conniption fit of fierce thrashing and squawking.

"Now, now, Sir Cedric," Sir Fartsalot whispered. He motioned toward the nest where Harry cowered in peril. "Perhaps we shouldn't make remarks that are insensitive to poultry."

"Ah, right you are," Sir Cedric said. "Sorry about that, Harry."

The giants, meanwhile, were quick to oblige Sir Cedric. Grog armed himself with a large boulder, while Blog found a long, clean-picked bone and brandished it like a club.

"Defend yourself, or selves, you wide-load, humungoloidal, glandular abnormalities!" Sir Cedric yelled, and set upon the giants with a dizzying display of swordsmanship: *Thrust, parry, thrust, thrust...*

Sir Cedric danced and weaved just out of the giants' reach. His sword slashed and flashed with dazzling flourish, with dashing finesse, carving the thin air to slivers. It was no match for him: *Thrust, parry, feint, thrust, thrust...*

Then, **CLANG!**

Blog clobbered him with his bone-club.

Sir Cedric's helmet rang like a gong. He staggered

this way. He stumbled that way. He teetered forward. He tottered back. Then, with a crash, he fell. Out cold.

"Oh, you're so butch!" Grog complimented.

Sir Fartsalot, meanwhile, had scrambled up the cliff-side to a ledge more at Blog and Grog's level. Now he called out in challenge: "On guard, giants!"

"Ooo, let's pound him to a pulpy plup!" suggested Grog.

"Let's smash him to a smooshy smudge!" said Blog.

They advanced on Sir Fartsalot.

Grog hefted the mighty boulder overhead.

Blog waved his deadly club.

Sir Fartsalot merely stooped and picked up a handful of sand.

"I'll clobber him to a glob of guts!"

"I'll mash him to a stain!"

Closer and closer the giants came, but Sir Fartsalot bravely stood his ground.

Grog growled.

Blog snarled.

Sir Fartsalot leaned on his swordhilt, whistling.

The giants towered directly over the brave old knight. Grog hoisted his boulder overhead to squash him. Blog drew back his bone-club to smite him.

But Sir Fartsalot made no move to dodge their blows or even raise his sword in self-defense. He merely flung his handful of sand at them, as calmly as if he was tossing a coin into a wishing well.

"Aargghh!" Grog squealed, clutching his eye in a sudden reflex.

"Ow!" Blog said, as the boulder Grog had dropped fell on his head. "Watch it, you big moron!"

"My eye!" Grog whined. "My eye!"

"Stuff your eye!" Blog said. He clubbed Grog on the noggin. "There, how do *you* like it?"

"OUCH! What was *that* for?"

Smack for whack and punch for crunch, things quickly escalated, until Sir Fartsalot was forgotten as Blog and Grog strove in combat with each other.

"Ow! Ow! Leggo my hair, you villain!"

"Den yet go uff my dose, doo youndrel!"

But even with the giants out of the way, Sir Fartsalot still had the bigger task before him of rescuing Harry from the terrible Tweety.

"Hang on, Prince Harry!" he called. "I'm coming!"

He leaped from ledge to ledge until he landed smack in the awful nest.

"Get back, foul fowl!" Sir Fartsalot warned, getting between the birdbeast and Prince Harry.

"Or I shall pluck thee wing from wing!"

Sir Fartsalot lunged with his sword. The roc shrank from its sting with squawks of pure fury. They circled each other, Sir Fartsalot on the attack, the birdbeast snapping its deadly beak at him as it edged away.

Again and again, Sir Fartsalot charged. Each time, the birdbeast hopped clear of his swordswipes, shrieking dark menace and pounding the nest with mighty wingbeats.

Sir Fartsalot lunged. The birdbeast sprang away.

He lunged again. The monster sprang up—
but this time came down right on top of him!

The roc seized Sir Fartsalot in its mighty talons. The
brave old knight struggled, but the fierce claws gripped
him tighter. The birdbeast shrieked and thrashed in
triumph, beating its outspread wings, so vast they
doubled its already alarming size.

Then, slowly, slowly, wings flapping like thunder, the
monster began to rise . . . It hovered a
moment over the nest . . . and then—

It was flying!

Up, up it went, dangling Sir Fartsalot like
a squirming rodent . . .

Then off, off, away from the cliff, off to the east, off among clouds ... toward the horizon ... soaring ... faraway ... gone ...

The giants stopped pounding each other to watch, spellbound. Tears came to their blackened eyes. They snuffled and wiped their bloodied noses on torn sleeves.

"They grow up so fast!" Blog sighed.

"Seems like only yesterday she was a sweet little egg ..." Grog said.

"Remember how we cradled her in our arms?"

"So worried we'd crack her ..."

"Now look at her ..."

"Flying!"

And the giants leaned their heads together, sobbing bittersweet sobs.

Harry, too, stared transfixed as Sir Fartsalot and the awful bird shrunk to a speck on the horizon, then disappeared beyond sight altogether. He kept staring long after, too, until sun and sky and clouds dissolved in a watery shimmer—for his eyes had filled with tears. *Oh, Sir Fartsalot!*

"Psst! Harry, over here!"

Sir Cedric had come to and was motioning Harry over to where the winged contraption lay.

Harry obeyed mechanically, too stunned with grief to think.

"Let's see," Sir Cedric said, strapping Harry in, "Sir Fartsalot did the steering, peace on his soul, but I think I can get the hang of it."

## 27

"How marvelous!" King Reginald exclaimed. "A choir of hummingbirds! Bees that can spell! Leaves that fall up! I wish somebody had told me years ago I had an Enchanted Forest in my Kingdom."

"Keep your voice down, Sire," Sir Bedwetter whispered. "The Mumbo Jumbos will hear you."

King Reginald rode at the head of a train of knights. Adventure and the open road had brought out the best in him. He was looking more kingly and commanding than ever. With him was a company of his finest knights: Sir Bedwetter, Sir Dulledge, Sir Thumbsucker, Sir Dainty, Sir Blunderdunce, Sir Bumbleclod, Sir Uttertwit, Sir Ticklish, Sir Nancy and Sir Bubba the Incontinent.

Suddenly, something gave Sir Bedwetter such a start that he almost jumped out of his saddle.

"Easy, man," the King said. "It's only your shadow."

It was true. Ever since the King's company entered the Enchanted Forest, Sir Bedwetter's shadow had been sneaking up on him, or jumping out at him, or looming over him from behind in large frightening shapes, until he was a nervous wreck.

"Well, it's not natural," Sir Bedwetter sulked, "lurking up on a person like that."

The King raised a hand and motioned for all to halt.

"Hark," he said. "Do you hear something?"

Sir Bedwetter, certain it was an ambush of Bugaboos, looked about in a panic for some place to hide.

From somewhere off among the trees, they heard a dim voice call: "Hello-o-o? ...Anybody there? ..."

"Don't answer, Sire," Sir Bedwetter warned. "It could be a trap!"

"A trap?" the King said.

"Phantasms," Sir Bedwetter explained. "Enchanted woods like these are full of them. They lure you off the path and then ..." He shivered and said no more, for it was too, too horrifying.

"Fiddle-faddle!" the King scoffed. He called out, "Who goes there?"

"Dad? ..." replied a different voice from the same direction. "Dad ... is that you?"

"Phantasms, my toe!" the King said. "Why, that's Prince Harry!"

"Wait!" Sir Bedwetter cautioned. "It could be phantasms *impersonating* the prince ..."

"If ye be friends, please hurry," called the first voice they had heard, "for we're in a bit of a spot of a fix."

The King steered his men toward the voices, over the objections of Sir Bedwetter, who only came along because he was even more afraid to be left behind in the Enchanted Forest.

They soon came to a mighty, ancient oak that towered like an elder over the smaller trees around it. Tangled high in its branches were Harry and Sir Cedric, still strapped in their marvelous glider.

They were lucky to be alive at all.

For back on the cliff, when Sir Cedric had lifted the great glider wings over them, they had dashed headlong off the edge of Mount Kaboom ...

Suddenly the ground had fallen away under their feet. The world was laid out beneath Harry like a scene woven into a carpet, and he had experienced the most exhilarating sensation of ... *flying*!

But this gave way almost immediately to an even more electrifying sensation of *dropping*.

For it turned out Sir Cedric didn't know how to steer the glider after all. They plummeted madly out of control and would have been smashed to bits, but at the last moment their glider veered and caught its wings in the branches of this tree. It was a miracle they were saved— and probably the doing of the Enchanted Forest itself.

That was yesterday. They had passed the night stuck in this tree. They were starving, thirsty and bursting, but none of that mattered to Harry. There was only one thought that filled his mind: *What had become of Sir Fartsalot?*

"Dad! It is you!" Harry said now, momentarily distracted from his misery. "What are you doing here?"

"I might ask you the same thing, young man," the King replied sternly.

Hanging by the glider straps across his chest, Harry appeared to be floating among the tree's upper leaves and branches.

"Stop your fooling and come down from there at once," the Kind commanded. "I want a word with you."

"We'd like to, Your Majesty," Sir Cedric said, hanging upside down. "Only we're stuck."

"Ah," the King remarked. "I see ...

"Men!" He ordered. "Chop, chop!"

The castle knights stared at the King, then at each other, then back at the King ...

"*Rescue* them!" the King explained.

"But how, Sire?" Sir Bedwetter replied. "You see yourself they are beyond our reach. Why, even if one of us on horseback were to stand on the shoulders of another man on horseback ..."

"So cut the tree down," the King suggested impatiently.

The trees around them shook and swayed as if in a violent gust. Sir Bedwetter ducked and winced and looked about in alarm.

"Shhh!" he urged, pressing a finger to his lips. "Sire, you know not what you say. Do you want to turn the whole forest against us?"

"Oh, all right," King Reginald grumbled. "Just climb up and snip them loose, then."

Sir Bedwetter stared at the mighty trunk's gnarled, upwending ascent. "Er, I would, Sire," he said. "But as an expert in the field of tree-climbing, I can tell you that this, uh, particular type of tree isn't suitable for climbing. Wouldn't support the extra weight."

"Then what do you propose?" the King demanded.

Sir Bedwetter frowned and scratched his head thoughtfully. Then he scratched his chin contemplatively. Then he scratched his armpits meditatively.

"In truth," he announced, "it seems hopeless."

"I think I have an idea," Sir Cedric interrupted. "But I shall need the supplest knight among you."

"Stand back, men," Sir Bedwetter commanded. "He means me."

"Indeed, you're the very man for the job," Sir Cedric agreed. "Come over here a moment," he directed. "No, closer...A bit to the left...That's perfect!"

Sir Bedwetter obeyed until he was standing directly under the tangled glider.

"Now what?" he asked.

With one neat slash of his sword, Sir Cedric cut himself loose from the straps that held him. He dropped head-first and would have broken his neck. But luckily Sir Bedwetter was there to cushion his fall.

"There's a chap," Sir Cedric thanked him as he got up.

"Oh, woe," moaned Sir Bedwetter, lying crushed in a heap. "Back...fractured...Spine...sprained..."

Slowly he peeled himself from the ground and struggled to his feet. He was feeling around for breaks and taking inventory of his bruises when Harry landed on him.

"Thanks, Bedwetter," Harry said. "My hero."

"Sir Cedric Knotaclew, I presume," King Reginald said

warmly. "We had heard that you'd joined Sir Fartsalot's quest. It's an honor to finally meet you."

"At your service, Your Majesty," Sir Cedric replied with a bow. "And the honor is mine."

There was a whinny, and out from behind the pack of knights stepped Codswallop! The great black stallion strode forward and nuzzled Sir Cedric's cheek.

"Aha!" the King said. "I guessed this was your mount when we found him wandering the woods with these two."

Fealty and Wildfire were there too, but neither of them rushed to greet Harry.

Harry didn't have time to wonder at this, though. He had bigger questions on his mind.

"Dad, what are you doing so far from the castle?"

"Looking for you," the King said crossly. "I know all about your little joke, young man. When Sir Bedwetter here told me, I set out at once to find you and save Sir Fartsalot from wasting any more of his time. Hunting boogers, indeed! You've made his name a laughingstock from here to the castle."

The King's words were a dagger in Harry's heart. Already full of grief about what had become of dear old Sir Fartsalot, he saw now that it had all come of his own stupid joke. Oh, what had he done! He had only meant it as a harmless prank!

"So," the King asked, looking about, "where *is* noble Sir Fartsalot?"

"Gone, I'm afraid," Sir Cedric answered solemnly. "Carried off by a roc. 'Tis a tale of valor and woe."

"Gone?" the King exclaimed. "You don't mean—?"

Sir Cedric nodded grimly.

"It's all my fault!" Harry bawled. "He was trying to save me!"

Harry buried his head in his hands and wept. Nobody tried to console him. Fealty wouldn't look at him, and even Wildfire kept his distance.

"At least he met his end in battle," Sir Cedric eulogized. "He would have wanted it that way."

28

With their search come to a dismal end, there was nothing for the King and his men to do but start back through the Enchanted Forest with heavy hearts.

And the heaviest by far belonged to Harry. Guilt and grief weighed on him like a great stone around his neck.

He was blind to the marvels of the Enchanted Forest. When Sir Bedwetter's shadow began pelting the nervous knight with squirrel droppings, it didn't even raise a snicker.

They had been riding in grim silence for some time when the King called a halt.

"Look," He pointed. "Yonder."

A plume of smoke rose over the trees ahead.

"Probably an ogre camp," Sir Cedric said. "We ran into a crowd of them not far from here."

Sir Bedwetter went suddenly pale.

"P-perhaps we should t-t-try another route," he stammered.

"Nonsense!" said Sir Cedric. "Arms ready, men!" Under his breath, he added, "This'll give these milk-fed castle knights a tale to spin over many a cozy castle evening to come!"

And with that, Sir Cedric gave Codswallop a tap with his heels and charged into the enemy camp. Harry spurred Wildfire to follow, not caring what happened to him.

But when they burst through the trees, there wasn't an ogre in sight. Just a cook fire. And roasting over it on a spit, a gigantic drumstick. And tending the flames ... "Sir Fartsalot!" Harry exclaimed. "You're alive!"

"Impossible!" Sir Cedric said. "I fear this apparition is but another of the forest's infernal tricks."

He reached out and pinched Sir Fartsalot's cheek to test if he was real or not. The old knight's fist flashed up and bopped him on the nose.

"Iddiz doo!" Sir Cedric cried out in delight, rubbing his nose.

"Of course it is," Sir Fartsalot said. "Er, sorry about that, old chap. Reflexes, you know."

Harry ran and hugged the dear old knight. Soon Fealty appeared beside him too, licking his master's face.

A moment later the King and his men arrived. Sir Bedwetter was the last to appear, stepping out from under a shrub.

"Er, I was laying in ambush," he explained.

"Laying in a bush!" grumbled the King. "And they call this the King's Army!"

"King Reginald!" Sir Fartsalot exclaimed. "My, this is a surprise! Will you and your men join me for dinner? There's plenty for all. I wish I could offer something more worthy of the occasion, but I'm afraid I set off in a bit of a rush yesterday without packing any turnips."

The King assured him there was no need to apologize. And really there wasn't.

What followed was the happiest feast in memory. The King's Men devoured the barbecued roc with hearty appetites, for they had journeyed many long late afternoons with nothing to drink but wine and nothing to eat but pastries, canapés and filet mignon.

Sir Fartsalot was overjoyed to see them all, especially Harry. He brought the King up to date on their travels since they left the castle, always exaggerating Harry's role in each adventure.

"Of course I was sorry to leave Sir Cedric in such a fix," he said when he had reached the last chapter of his tale. "But I knew Harry here would dispatch those giants and get him out okay. I tell you, Your Majesty, the young prince has the makings of a knight of the rarest skill and bravery."

The old knight's eyes shone fondly on his protégé, which made Harry feel even lower than he did already.

"Yes, mark my words," Sir Fartsalot went on, "someday the feats of *Sir Harry of Armpit* will be famous throughout the land." He gave 'Sir Harry' a wink. "But enough bragging about our adventures, eh, Harry? Tell me, Good King, what brings you to these accursed woods?"

The atmosphere changed instantly. All the gaiety left the party. Even the King's knights almost paused in eating.

"Well, Sir Fartsalot," the King said. "To tell you the truth, we bring some unpleasant news ..."

Harry hung his head. A tear rolled down his cheek.

But suddenly, something else distracted everyone's attention.

"Alack!" Sir Fartsalot cried, jumping to his feet and drawing his sword.

"Ugh!" said the others, and, "P.U.!"

"The Foul West Wind!" Sir Fartsalot said, for so it was. "It can mean but one thing: The Booger is near at hand!"

The company exchanged looks over pinched noses.

Sir Fartsalot ran about barking orders:

"King Reginald, you and five of your finest men scour the forest thither...Sir Bedwetter and some of the leftover knights, look yon...the dregs of the group can follow Sir Cedric thataway . . . Prince Harry, search thisaway with me..."

Nobody moved.

"Quick! To horse!" the old knight urged. "If you spy the beast, make a signal like this—" Sir Fartsalot put one hand under his armpit and made three loud honks. "We will encircle the monster and cut off its escape. But be careful, men—it's extremely dangerous when cornered."

"Harry," the King said sternly, "tell him."

Sir Fartsalot continued shouting orders and making hurrying up gestures with his sword.

"Tell him," the King repeated.

His Majesty glared at Harry.

"*Tell him.*"

"Oh, all right," Sir Fartsalot sighed. He saw he would get nowhere until they'd said their say. "Tell me *what*?"

"I'm so sorry!" Harry bawled. Tears streamed down his face.

Sir Fartsalot was bewildered.

Then Sir Bedwetter butted in, only too happy to explain.

"This Booger you've been after is a hoax," he gloated. "A fraud. A mere figment of the prince's overactive imagination. You see, this whole quest of yours was just one of his little jokes. What a booger *really* is, I don't even have the heart to tell you."

Then, with a smirk, he told him.

Sir Fartsalot was speechless.

"Is this true, Harry?" he said, not wanting to believe it (and still speechless when he'd finished speaking).

Harry just buried his head in his hands. Sir Fartsalot looked to Sir Cedric for his opinion.

"I did suspect as much, Sir Farty," he said gloomily.

Sir Fartsalot's sword fell to his side. His shoulders sagged. All his years seemed to catch up with him in an instant. He looked suddenly old and worn out.

"If you'll excuse me," he said, "methinks I will retire from your party. Suddenly I find I am too old for questing. Hereafter, I shall find me a damp dark cave somewhere and live out the rest of my days as a hermit, far from the laughing eyes of the world."

And with that, the old knight hobbled away down the path, leaning on his sword like a cane. Fealty gave Harry a dirty look and followed.

29

They all sat in gloomy silence, staring down the path where Sir Fartsalot had disappeared. Even the King's men were so overcome with emotion that some of them had to put their forks down momentarily.

"There goes the bravest knight who ever swung the sword," Sir Cedric said.

"'Tis a great loss," the King agreed. "Harry, I may have been blind to your faults in the past, but this time you've done a terrible thing."

There was no need for the King to scold, for Harry had never felt worse. He would have given anything to take back what he had done. Seeing Sir Fartsalot broken and disgraced, and knowing how he valued his honor above all else, Harry wondered if the old knight might've been happier if he *had* perished in battle with the roc.

"Well," said Sir Bedwetter, breaking the grim silence, "if nobody's going to eat that last wing..."

What happened next, none of them would ever forget. A horrible noise ripped the air—a long, liquidy backsnort, like someone trying to inhale a raw egg through a straw, but loud as thunder.

The King's knights looked at each other in alarm, calculating who was the slowest among them and would be first caught if they tried to flee.

Then they heard it again, coming from down the path.

"Sir Fartsalot!" Harry gasped. "He's in trouble!"

He jumped to his feet and dashed toward the horrible noise, with Sir Cedric at his heels. King Reginald followed, herding his skittish knights before him.

Nothing in Harry's adventures so far could have prepared him for what they found.

There before them was the most hideous monster ever imagined: a mighty, shapeless blob, bigger than a castle, and made entirely of a slimegreen goo so horrible that even a speck of it would make anyone shrink in disgust.

"'Snot—" gasped the King in disbelief.

"'Tis!" said another voice, from the back.

The blob mountain roared and raged. Brave Sir Fartsalot charged at it on horseback, slashing it with his sword, then rode off to regroup for another attack.

"'Snot—" the King repeated. "Surely it can't be—"

"But 'tis!" said the other voice. "Just look at it."

Whenever Sir Fartsalot charged, the creature reared back from his slashing blade like an elephant afraid of a mouse. But each time the brave old knight retreated, the thing advanced steadily after him, oozing like a slug.

"It's a—" said the King.

"A—" said Sir Cedric.

"A—" said Harry.

"*AH CHOO*!!!" the creature bellowed, and flung a glop of green slime at Sir Fartsalot. He ducked as it flew past his shoulder ...

There was a *splat* and a pitiful wail. Sir Bedwetter lay immobilized under an oozing heap of green slimegoo.

"Ma-a-a-a-m-a-a-a-!" he moaned.

"It's a Booger!" said the voice at the back. "The infamous, dreaded Booger!"

Something familiar about the voice made Harry turn ...

And there, perched in a tree, was the owl that had saved him in the Enchanted Forest!

The owl was right, too. That glistening tower of slime was indeed the creature Sir Fartsalot had so long sought.

"Then there is such a thing," said the King. "And we were all sure it was only in Sir Fartsalot's imagination."

The owl winked at Harry.

"Well, I'll be," said Sir Cedric.

Sir Fartsalot galloped around and around the beast, slashing at it with every pass and spattering goo everywhere. But the gashes his sword made filled in immediately and left no wounds, and the creature gave no sign of weakening.

"Shouldn't we try to rescue him?" asked the King.

"Rescue him?" Sir Cedric replied. "Are you kidding? Look at him; he's having the time of his life. Why, he looks like a young man of sixty-five again."

It was true. Sir Fartsalot beamed with joy, and obviously his strength and spirit had returned. Gone was the sad, broken old man they had seen just a few minutes before.

But too late did they realize the vile monster was herding Sir Fartsalot into a trap. For each time the brave knight charged and retreated, the Booger steered him toward a rocky hill. Now the creature had Sir Fartsalot backed up against the hillside—cornered!

Sir Fartsalot saw he was cut off and dismounted for a final stand. He sent Fealty away with a slap on the flank and made one last charge on foot to keep the Booger busy while she escaped.

He attacked the goo monster with a furious flurry of swordswipes, slashing left, then right, then left again ... The beast reared up, shrinking from the sting of his blade ...

But then the Booger reached out a slimy tentacle of goo. It looped around and around Sir Fartsalot, then tightened like a snare ...

The old knight fought and struggled, but the Booger snatched him up in its gooey grasp and began oozing slugwise toward a huge cave in the side of the hill.

"Oh, no!" Sir Cedric gasped. "If that thing gets him into its lair, he's done for!"

"Quick, men," the King ordered. "We must stop the creature!"

They charged, firing a hail of arrows that stuck in the Booger's sides but didn't slow it.

Harry and the others were left to watch in horror as the Booger disappeared into its cave, leaving a trail of green slime.

"Noooo!!!" Harry screamed. He tried to run, but someone had a grip on his shoulder.

"We're too late, Harry!" Sir Cedric said grimly. "It's between Sir Fartsalot and the monster now. Whatever happens, this was how he wanted it."

Thunderous noises echoed from deep within the cave: loud sucking sniffles and slurpy backsnorts so piteous they made the most fearless among them wince and cringe. Finally, the cave exploded in a mighty honk that shook the ground as if the very earth itself was blowing into a hanky ...

Then the cave fell silent.

Dead silent.

They all stared at the entrance, too stunned to speak. Harry looked to Sir Cedric, and the tears in the knight's eyes were all the explanation he needed.

## 30

A moment later, though, a figure appeared in the cave's entrance. It had the shape of a man but seemed to be made of boogerslime from head to foot.

"Run away!" shouted Sir Bedwetter. "It's the spawn of the Booger!"

The figure staggered toward them, moving stiffly, like a zombie ... It clutched at its head as if to wrench it from its own neck ...

Then off popped his helmet, and they saw it was Sir Fartsalot!

"The Booger is no more," he announced, dripping with slimegoo.

"Run away anyway!" urged Sir Bedwetter. "Yuck!"

Harry and the others all circled around Sir Fartsalot—without getting too close.

Harry didn't rush to hug the old knight this time, but praised him from afar.

"You were incredible!" he said.

Even Fealty just sort of whinnied her appreciation from the wings.

"Hurrah for brave Sir Fartsalot!" the King cheered. "He has rid the kingdom of the vile Booger!"

Everyone agreed it was the most heroic deed in the history of knighthood.

Amid all the hubbub and celebration, nobody but Harry saw a tiny grey kitten emerge from the mouth of the cave, where it sat washing its fur.

But that was not the end of the surprises that day. For now the owl, which nobody but Harry had noticed in all the excitement, flew down and—with a *pop!* and a puff of smoke—appeared before them in the form of a man dressed in wizard's robes.

"Permit me to introduce myself," he said with a deep bow. "I am Randalf the Wizard."

"I say, Sir Cedric," Sir Fartsalot said, "doesn't that chap in the cloud of smoke look familiar?"

"Why, he's the very twin of the mad inventor who gave us that infernal glider," Sir Cedric agreed.

Harry recognized him too—but as the Fool who had put them on the path to Knockon Wood.

"I must warn you," the wizard said, "you have stumbled into an Enchanted Forest. This is a perilous place, full of dangerous magic—as some in your party have already found out."

The wizard winked at Harry.

"But if you follow that trail," he said, pointing to a path that Harry was sure hadn't been there a few minutes before, "it will lead you out of the Enchanted Forest and back the way you came. In fact, I'm heading that way myself, so why don't I join you?"

• • •

And whether by some magic of his own or the forest's, or possibly just by one of those shortcuts stories take when they are winding up, the wizard led them out of the Enchanted Forest in no time at all. Soon the path widened and became again the Open Road—and a sign marked "Home" pointed them on their way.

"Thank you for your help, Sir Wizard," said the King. "Is there any way I can repay you? I am a King of considerable means, you know."

"I have no need for gold or riches," said the wizard. "But there is one favor you might grant me. Lately I find my work has become too much for me and I need an apprentice. I've been watching the young prince here for some time now, and I think he may possess a certain gift for invention…"

"Wow! Can I, Dad?" Harry gushed. But then he caught himself. "No," he said. "I mean, I think I'd rather stay on as Sir Fartsalot's squire instead. That is, if he'll still have me…"

"Harry, I would be honored," Sir Fartsalot said merrily. "But I'm afraid I stand by my decision to hang up my sword. I plan to retire to a quiet life on a little plot of land with Fealty and our new addition here."

The "new addition" was a kitten Sir Fartsalot had just adopted back in the Enchanted Forest. He had found it near the entrance to the fateful cave and named it "Wee Booger" as a joke.

"Take the wizard's offer, Harry," Sir Fartsalot said. "I have a hunch he may be right about your talents."

But King Reginald wasn't sure it was such a good idea.

"I'm afraid you would regret it," the King warned the wizard. "He'd cause you no end of trouble."

"No, Dad, I've learned my lesson," Harry promised. "I know now that pranks don't always turn out the way you plan."

31

**W**ord that Sir Fartsalot had slain the awful Booger spread quickly throughout the kingdom. All along the road back to the castle, the old knight was greeted as a hero. Peasants came out of their huts to gawk at him, and travelers passing on the road asked for his autograph. And all of them said how *they'd* always believed in his quest, back when others were calling him a loony, even if they hadn't exactly come out and said so at the time.

Now that he was retired, Sir Fartsalot went off his questing diet. He ate everything put in front of him, like a starving man who hadn't tasted food in weeks.

"I don't care if I ever see another turnip," he mumbled one evening at dinner, through a mouthful of elderberry pie.

And never a whiff was whiffed of the Foul West Wind in that kingdom again, which goes to show that the Booger must have been the cause of it after all.

The King and his knights took the long road back to the castle, down every side-road and detour. His Majesty was living out his boyhood dream, roaming the land in search of adventures.

And he found them, too. He and his knights tangled with an angry cave Cyclops on the rampage after they disturbed its nap. They barely escaped being baked into pies and tarts when a witch disguised as a roadside pastry chef sold them chocolate éclairs spiked with sleeping potion. And they were nearly gobbled up by a mighty lake serpent but got the better of the beast by scrambling valiantly to shore and bravely taking the long way around.

They never got a good look at the serpent, for it was hidden underwater, but the knights all agreed it must have been as big as a castle. That is, until one of them suggested that in fact it was as big as *two* castles. And then they had to admit it probably was. And then, the more they thought about it, pretty soon they realized the monster actually had to be as big as twenty castles if it was an inch.

They came through most of these adventures none

the worse, but His Majesty did lose a few good men while passing the castle of the lovesick princesses. He didn't mind, though, for in truth they weren't all *that* good.

Sir Cedric rode with them part of the way but then took his leave. He claimed he'd heard rumors of some Hollow Pretext running amok in a remote corner of the Kingdom. But Harry suspected the truth was he feared to venture back into the princesses' territory after his last narrow escape.

As for Harry, he began his lessons with Randalf the Wizard during the long journey home. In no time at all he had learned spells to make things fly, or disappear, or appear suddenly out of nowhere, or turn into something else altogether. Whatever the wizard thought he saw in Harry, he must have been right, for the young prince turned out to have quite a knack.

And so everyone lived happily ever after.

Everyone, that is, except Sir Bedwetter. From the time they finally returned to the castle, he was plagued by a series of bizarre accidents. Once, in the middle of a jousting match, some mysterious force—people said it must have been the wind—lifted him right out of his saddle and dropped him in a nearby pigsty. Another time, he reached for his sword hilt and found himself grabbing a live snake instead! (He was petrified of snakes.) But worst of all was the time he rode out proudly for a tournament match, only to have the crowds burst out laughing. He looked down and discovered his armor had disappeared, and he was sitting on his horse in his underwear!

One morning not long after, he was in the castle courtyard telling Lady Dimplewit about the time he rescued Sir Fartsalot from a band of ogres back in the Enchanted Forest.

"I had just a handful of knights with me," he said. "And there were probably a hundred ogres hidden all over that forest. But they must have fled in terror when they saw that I was in command."

"Who, the knights?" asked Lady Dimplewit.

"No, the ogres," said Sir Bedwetter.

"Weren't you afraid?" she asked.

"Madam, I don't know what fear is," Sir Bedwetter

said. "I have trained myself to fight as the eagle or the lion does, by instinct and reflex alone."

Suddenly from behind them came an enormous roar: "RRRRRRRRR—"

Too loud for a dragon, it had to be something incredibly huge and ferocious. Sir Bedwetter's instincts kicked in immediately: He dove behind Lady Dimplewit's skirts, covered his eyes, and trembled.

"RRRrrrribbit!"

Actually, it was just a bullfrog. And not even a very big one.

"Yo, Bedwetter," said Harry, appearing behind them. "Nice reflexes."

Harry lifted the bullfrog and cupped it in his hands.

"Bad Ferdinand," he scolded. "Haven't I told you not to pop up on people?"

Sir Bedwetter scowled at Harry in black fury.

"Sir Bedwetter, what are you doing down there?"

It was the King. With him was a large audience of knights, advisors, and other castle folk. They all stared at Sir Bedwetter with scandalized looks.

"Ah, good morning, Harry," said the King. "Working hard at your studies, I hope?"

"You bet," Harry said. "Why, I can't tell you half the things I've been doing."

"There's a good boy," said the King.

"You see," His Majesty added to Sir Bedwetter, as if settling an old argument. "I always said that all the prince needed was a hobby to keep him out of trouble."

**B**ut as for Sir Fartsalot, it wasn't long before Harry began to hear reports that the old knight was having trouble settling into his retirement. Rumors reached the castle that he was restless and bored, being used to a life of more activity. There was talk that his neighbors were beginning to worry about him.

Harry decided to investigate for himself, so he went to visit his old friend.

On the road to Sir Fartsalot's new home, Harry came upon a peasant woman. She was staring out into a field of vegetables with an angry look on her face.

"Drat that gopher!" she cursed. "He's in at my rutabagas again!"

The gopher was sitting upright in the vegetable patch.

It nibbled a bit of rutabaga from one paw, then sampled a bite of spring onion from the other.

"Fear not, madam!" called a voice Harry knew well. "I will defend your fields from this furry scourge!"

Harry turned to see dear old Sir Fartsalot barreling downhill on Fealty with his lance lowered...

They galloped through the vegetable patch. Sir Fartsalot's lance tore up a long row of vegetables.

When he had passed, the rutabagas were all uprooted, the squash were squashed, and the peas were in pieces. But the gopher was unharmed.

"I have flushed him from his cover," Sir Fartsalot announced. "Now I shall finish him off."

He wheeled Fealty around and made another charge. His lance whammed into some yams and turned up a row of turnips. The gopher ducked down a hole just before it struck him.

Sir Fartsalot galloped out the far side of the vegetable patch and turned Fealty around once more. The beets were beat up. The beans looked like they'd been punched in the kidneys. And the peas all had black eyes.

The gopher poked its head up out of another hole, munching a carrot.

"I see I have underestimated you, my worthy foe," Sir Fartsalot said. "But now you shall taste the wrath of ... Lucille!"

The old knight swept out his sword and jumped down from his saddle. He rushed into the vegetable patch, slashing left and right, garroting carrots and tomahawking tomatoes. But the gopher kept dodging down holes and popping up out of other ones all over the garden.

When Sir Fartsalot was through, the vegetable patch looked like a tossed salad. Except in places where it looked more like a gazpacho. The leeks had all sprung leaks. The radishes were looking baddish. The spinach was finached.

The gopher was nowhere in sight.

"I'm afraid the scoundrel has escaped, madam," Sir Fartsalot said, sheathing his sword. "But I daresay he'll think twice before coming back."

The peasant woman was too overcome with emotion (gratitude, probably) to reply. She just spluttered and tore her hair in thanks.

"Why, hello, Prince Harry!" Sir Fartsalot said in surprise. He clasped Harry warmly in greeting. "What an unexpected pleasure!"

"I dropped by to see how you were doing," Harry explained.

"Oh, fine," Sir Fartsalot said. "Keeping busy."

Sir Fartsalot showed Harry back to his hut. It was small but cozy, with a fireplace for cooking, a table with a pair of chairs, and a soft warm bed in the corner. (Though after all his years on the road, Sir Fartsalot preferred to sleep on the floor underneath it.)

But what struck Harry first was the overpowering smell when he stepped inside—and the strange objects hanging from the ceiling.

"Ugh!" Harry commented. Then (pinching his nose), "What are doze?"

"Cheeses," Sir Fartsalot said proudly, laying one on

the table. "Now that I'm free to eat whatever I want, I've been making my own gourmet cheeses: Limburger, blue cheese, Gorgonzola..."

There was a loud noise as Sir Fartsalot cut the cheese. A blast of odor wafted up into Harry's face.

"Here, try some," the old knight said, offering Harry a sliver of Gorgonzola on the end of his knife.

For more than an hour, they talked about their adventures old and new, with Sir Fartsalot pausing every so often to cut the cheese.

It was a nice visit, but when it was finally time to go, Harry was glad to step out into the fresh air again. Sir Fartsalot walked him outside.

A woman appeared in the doorway of the hut next door.

"Staaan-ley!" she called out. "That rat's been in at the larder ag–"

The woman saw Sir Fartsalot and clammed up in mid-sentence.

"What is that you say, madam?" Sir Fartsalot asked.

"Er, nothing," the woman said. "No problems here, Sir Knight."

"A rat, eh?" Sir Fartsalot said.

"Oh, er, he's no bother, really," she insisted. "Almost

like a pet, you might say...Practically one of the family..."

"Stand aside, my dear lady," Sir Fartsalot said boldly. "I will take care of that rascal."

He strode over to her hut, brandishing his sword.

"On guard, rat!" Sir Fartsalot called out, disappearing into the doorway. "I'll teach you to steal from these honest folk. Have at you!"

There was a loud *thwack!* of splintering wood, and a **CRASH!** of smashing crockery...

Then another **CRASH!**

And another *thwack!*

And a BOOMF! of some large furniture item collapsing on a dirt floor...

Harry smiled, relieved to find his old friend settling so well into retirement after all, and set off home toward the castle.

## ACKNOWLEDGMENTS

Many thanks to all the people whose efforts have made this book so much better than it was: Ben Schrank for boldly pulling out all the stops, Kristin Smith for her inspired design, Stephen for the awesome pictures, and Jessica Rothenberg for pulling everything together. And of course to Faith Hamlin, my agent and publishing guru, for making it all happen.

Thanks also to students at First Avenue Public School, who taught me everything and were my inspiration. Hope you like it.

**KEVIN BOLGER** is a writer, teacher, and kid lit aficionado (that's *spanish* for "geek") in Ottawa, Canada. He has taught reading and writing to children for close to ten years. He is the author of *Sir Fartsalot Hunts The Booger* and *Zombiekins*. Visit **www.SirFartsalot.com** to find out more!

**STEPHEN GILPIN** has been working as an illustrator and cartoonist since 2000 and has nearly twenty picture books and chapter books under his belt. Gilpin is known for *Sneezy the Snowman*, *Even Firefighters Go to the Potty*, *Pirate Mom*, *100 Snowmen*, and more.

# Kevin Bolger

# Illustrated by Aaron Blecha

RAZORBILL

**RAZORBILL**

An Imprint of Penguin Random House LLC
Penguin.com

RAZORBILL & colophon is a registered trademark
of Penguin Random House LLC.

First published in the United States of America by Razorbill,
an imprint of Penguin Random House LLC, 2010

LIBRARY OF CONGRESS CATALOGING-IN-PUBLICATION DATA IS AVAILABLE

Razorbill ISBN 978-1-59514-177-4
This omnibus edition ISBN 978-1-98483-661-8

Printed in the United States of America

1 3 5 7 9 10 8 6 4 2

This one's for you, Mom.

—K. B.

For Nicky, my zombie bride

—A. B.

**THE LITTLE TOWN OF DEMENTEDYVILLE WAS A TIDY,**
uneventful town. The sort of place where home
owners took care never to let their well-tended lawns
become overrun by unsightly weeds or children, and
birds sang in all the trees—but only between the
hours of nine and five, as per the town's bylaws.

But even in Dementedyville there was one house
that stood out from all the others....

Number 4 Shadow Lane, the Widow Imavitch's place, was so spooky that children dared one another to go trick-or-treating to the door each Halloween. But nobody ever did. Naturally everyone believed the place was haunted. And then, of course, there were the strange stories about the Widow herself....

Most of these rumors were started by Reuben Rumpelfink, the Widow's neighbor. He was always complaining about her eccentric ways: About the weeds that grew wild in her garden, which he claimed had tried to eat his dog. About the bonfire parties she held whenever there was a full moon, where her guests (disreputable characters of questionable grooming habits) carried on loudly from midnight to sunrise. And about the mysterious storm cloud that hung over her yard in every kind of weather.

"That woman is a freak!" Mr. Rumpelfink told anyone who would listen. "She's a danger to us all!"

The day this story begins, Mr. Rumpelfink was leading a frenzied mob of townspeople up Shadow Lane, heading straight for the Widow's gates. Some of the crowd carried pitchforks, or axes, or flaming torches. Their faces were set in looks of fierce determination, as if they had some grim purpose in mind and would let nothing stand in their way....

News of a sale had spread all over town in minutes. People dropped whatever they were doing and rushed right over. Nobody wanted to miss out on any deals.

As the bargain-crazed mob surged toward the Widow's laneway, the gates suddenly swung open, *as if by magic....*

"Probably just motion sensors," Miranda told her friend Stanley Nudelman. "Why do you always have to go imagining things?"

Stanley and Miranda walked home this way from school every day.

"Let's go take a look," Miranda said. "I bet the Widow has lots of cool stuff."

"I'm not sure that's such a good idea," Stanley hesitated. "You know what people say about her...."

"Don't tell me you actually believe all those dumb rumors?" Miranda scoffed. "Come on, Stanley. Just because somebody lives in a spooky old house, and wears black all the time, and has a toad for a pet, and keeps a broomstick chained to a bicycle rack by her door, and talks to bats, and appears and disappears mysteriously wherever a certain black cat is around, *that doesn't make her a witch*."

But Stanley was not the kind of boy who liked taking chances.

"I don't know...." he fretted.

"Oh, come on," Miranda said. "What's the worst thing that could happen?"

**ONCE STANLEY AND**
Miranda were inside
the gates, the Widow's
sale was a big disappoint-
ment. There was noth-
ing particularly strange or
mysterious about the items
she was selling. It was just
a bunch of kitchen

stuff, old clothes, puzzles that were missing
pieces, a cracked wardrobe mirror,
some dusty old furniture—the
same junk you always find at
yard sales. Except the Widow's
mirror had a ghost in it and all
her chairs bit.

13

The Widow herself was nowhere in sight, but her cat seemed to be following them. It kept winding in and out of their legs, purring.

Miranda crouched down to pet it. But Stanley just said "Nice kitty" without getting too close because he was allergic.

Mr. Rumpelfink was there too, hunched over a pad of paper, scribbling furtive notes as he moved from table to table inspecting the items for sale.

"I wonder what *he's* doing here?" Stanley said.

"Snooping, probably," Miranda guessed. "I bet he's trying to find something he can use against the Widow.

"Hey, speaking of Mr. Rumpelfink," said Miranda, "doesn't this pincushion look just like him?"

She held up a homemade doll with shiny silver pins stuck into it. It really did look a lot like Mr. Rumpelfink. Miranda turned the doll over in her hands, pulling the pins in and out, in and out.

"Weird," Stanley agreed. But something else had caught his eye....

It was some sort of stuffed animal, still in its box. Only it wasn't like any stuffed animal Stanley had ever seen before....

It had one floppy bunny ear on a teddy bear's head and body...webbed paws with sharp claws... feet like a lizard...and two fangs instead of a rabbit's buckteeth.

Its eyes were sewn on like buttons—one fixed straight ahead with a cold, blank stare, the other dangling on a loose thread. Its fur was mangled and matted. And even still in the box, it was covered in cobwebs.

Something about the strange toy appealed to Stanley. It was so different from his kid sister's annoying stuffed animals, with their treacly songs and their adorable remarks whenever you squeezed their tummies.

"Check this out," Stanley said, showing Miranda. "I think I might buy it."

"Purrr-fect," mewled a voice. It was Mrs. Imavitch. She must've been standing behind them all along— how could they not have noticed her? "Zat is a *most* remarkable toy."

"Y-yeah, it's, uh, pretty freaky...." Stanley said, a little rattled by her popping up out of nowhere. "I bet everyone at school would think it's cool."

"Ah, yes, that could cause *qvuite* a sensation," the Widow said mysteriously. "It might give your schoolmates a bit of excitement some of zem vould never forget—*and some vould never remember....*"

"Huh?" Stanley asked. She was starting to creep him out a little. "W-what do you mean?"

"My dear, zat is no ordinary toy," the Widow started to explain. "It's—"

But then, noticing Mr. Rumpelfink eavesdropping on them from behind a rack of black and off-black robes, she paused mid-sentence.

"...*full of surprises*," the Widow said at last, with a very speaking look. Then she whispered, "*Just be sure to read zee instructionz.*"

"Vait here," the Widow added, then disappeared in the direction of her house.

"Boy, no wonder people think she's weird," Miranda said. "What do you think *that* was all about?"

"I don't know," Stanley said, suddenly having second thoughts about his new toy. "Do you think maybe it's cursed or something?"

Miranda just rolled her eyes.

"Stanley, for the hundredth time, there's no such thing as curses and witches and all that silly voodoo stuff," she said, flinging the pincushion back onto the table.

A minute later, Mrs. Imavitch returned with a bag of leftover Halloween candy— taffy, the kind no one liked, wrapped in waxed paper covered with silhouettes of vampire bats and witches on broomsticks.

Stanley tried to politely turn down the wretched candy, but the Widow kept pressing it on him.

"Take it," she urged, with more strange looks. "You never know vhen it might come in handy. I never get any trick-or-treaters at my place anyvay," the Widow added. "I guess kids today just aren't into Halloween like zey vere in my day."

Stanley took the taffy and paid for Zombiekins. By now he just wanted to get out of there. But even as he was leaving with Miranda, the Widow called after him one last time, "*Don't forget to read zee instructionz!*"

**3**

**BUT OF COURSE STANLEY NEVER DID READ THE**
instructions. He took Zombiekins out
of its box and threw the packag-
ing in a trashcan before
he reached the end
of the block.
But he kept the
taffy in his knap-
sack because he
was afraid to offend
the Widow by throw-

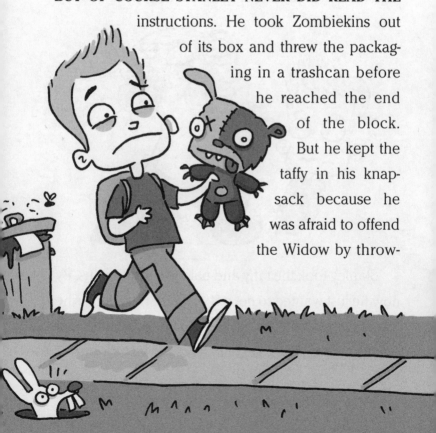

ing it out. Miranda said he was crazy to think she'd ever know, but there was something mysterious about the Widow, and Stanley was not the kind of boy who liked taking chances.

Stanley walked up the lane to his house wondering, what was so special about his new toy. What had the Widow been trying to tell him?

The sound of the front door opening brought Stanley's dog Fetch barking from the far end of the house. Fetch came bounding around the corner to meet Stanley with his tail wagging his whole body like a rubber noodle.

But when Fetch saw what Stanley was holding he skidded to a halt, knocking a potted geranium off an end table. His tail drooped between his legs. He started yelping and backpedaling wildly, knocking over the end table, then disappeared back around the corner as quickly as he'd come.

"Some watchdog," Stanley chuckled.

"*Stanley, dear,*" his mother called from the kitchen, "*can you check on your sister?*"

Stanley found his two-year-old sister Rosalie in the TV room. She was dressed in her princess costume and busy building a wobbly castle out of the good china, a pair of crystal vases, her mother's wedding dress, open paint cans, sharp objects, broken glass, a box marked FIREWORKS, and miscellaneous electrical hazards.

"*It's okay, Mom,*" Stanley called back reassuringly. "*She's in here.*"

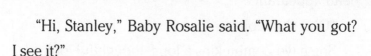

"Hi, Stanley," Baby Rosalie said. "What you got? I see it?"

She grabbed Zombiekins out of Stanley's hands

23

before he could answer. There was a low growl from under the couch where Fetch h a d taken cover.

"Ooo, him *scary*," Rosalie said.

"Yeah, well, it's sort of a 'zombie' stuffed animal," Stanley explained.

"'Zombie'?" Rosalie said. "Why him 'zombie'?"

Uh-oh. How was Stanley going to answer that one? He didn't want to scare her. But, on the other hand, he didn't believe in sheltering her from the facts of life, either.

"Well, a zombie is a reanimated corpse that's been revivified by witchcraft or transformed by the bite of another zombie," Stanley explained.

Rosalie stared back at him blankly.

"But don't worry," Stanley added, "this isn't a *real* zombie. It's just a stuffy with a sort of macabre, half-dead appearance."

"Oh," she replied.

She gave Zombiekins a long, thoughtful look.

"Him still scary," she concluded at last.

**AN HOUR LATER, STANLEY WAS IN THE MIDDLE OF** doing his homework when Fetch appeared in his bedroom doorway, barking at him.

"Not now, Fetch," Stanley said. "I'm too busy doing homework to play with you."

"Woof!" Fetch barked again, more urgently. "Woof! Woof!"

Most people assumed Fetch was dumb just because he was always doing things like licking frozen fire hydrants and peeing on the rug. But Stanley knew Fetch was smarter than everybody thought. If only his family had named him Fido or Spot, maybe he wouldn't have flunked out of obedience school and things might've been different. As it was, no wonder the poor dog had been confused with everybody yelling "Sit, Fetch!" and "Stay, Fetch!" and "No, Fetch—NOT ON THE TEACHER'S SHOE!!!" at him all the time.

Fetch barked again, then pointed with his paw down the hall. For some reason, Stanley got the feeling Fetch was trying to tell him something.

"What is it, boy?" Stanley asked. "Are you trying to tell me something?"

Fetch put his front paws to his throat and rolled on the ground like he was choking himself. Then he stood on his hind legs and walked with his front paws stretched out before him like Frankenstein. Then he pointed down the hall again.

Fetch *was* trying to tell him something—Stanley was almost sure of it.

"What is it, boy?" Stanley asked again

Fetch sighed and rolled his eyes. Even Lassie's family was never *this* thick. Finally the dog gave up and took Stanley's hand in his mouth.

"Do you want me to follow you?" Stanley asked as Fetch dragged him out into the hall. "Is that it, boy?"

Fetch led Stanley down the hall and stopped outside the playroom door. Stanley could hear strange noises coming from the other side—a sort of strangled gurgling sound....

Slowly, he turned the knob...pushed the door open...and...

SOMETHING JUMPED OUT AT HIM!!!

It had dead sunken eyes—gray rotting flesh—blood dripping from a mouth full of fangs—a pink sequined dress with matching tiara—

Stanley jumped back. Fetch yelped and peed on the carpet.

"Look, Stanley," the ghoulish apparition said, "I a zombie princess!"

It was Baby Rosalie, wearing an old rubber Halloween mask with her princess outfit.

"I having a tea party!" she said. Then, with a strangled gurgling sound, she pretended to sip tea from an empty teacup.

Seated at a doll's tea table on the playroom floor was Zombiekins. Across the table was Whimsy the Pfoo, a teddy of his sister's that went around wearing nothing but a sweater.

"Hugs are cuddle-wonderful," Whimsy announced. "Have a huggsy-wuggsy day...."

Zombiekins just sat there silently, one eye fixed straight ahead and the other hanging loosely by a thread.

Stanley looked at Fetch. Maybe his dog *was* pretty dumb after all. He turned to go back to his room— and suddenly felt something warm and wet soaking through his sock....

**THAT NIGHT, WHILE STANLEY AND HIS FAMILY WERE** sleeping in their beds, something strange and unexpected happened in the playroom....

The room was dark and eerily quiet. Nothing stirred but a curtain that shivered now and then in a cold night draft. In the deep midnight stillness, the ticking of a clock down the hall seemed to echo like a banging gavel through the upstairs rooms. (And it was a digital clock.) A full moon shone in through the window, and as it rose in the sky, hour by hour, a shaft of moonlight crept slowly across the floor. . . .

Until in the deepest, darkest part of the night, its moonglow shone at last on a heap of toys in a corner. . . .

Something stirred in the depths of the pile. Suddenly the toys at the top were pushed aside. . . . And something . . . began to emerge . . . from underneath. . . .

Somewhere, a scream of terror ripped through the night. . . .

(Not in this story, mind you, but *somewhere*.)

And then, from under the pile of toys, Zombiekins slowly arose. One eye was fixed straight ahead in a cold blank stare, the other lolled sidelong toward the floor. A strange voice rang out in the dark:

"*Oooo, I feel huggily-snuggily.*"

It was Whimsy, still sitting on his frumpy rump at the tidy tea table.

Zombiekins started to cross the room, walking stiffly and with a limp—one leg swiveling on its teddy-bear joint, the other dragging like a dead limb....

**Stump!—scri-i-i-i-itch** ... **Stump!—scri-i-i-i-itch** ... **Stump!—scri-i-i-i-itch** ...

Slowly and steadily, Zombiekins advanced across the playroom, driven by some dark, unknown purpose.

"A hug a day keeps the frownies away...." Whimsy enthused.

**Stump!—scri-i-i-i-i-itch** ...
**Stump!—scri-i-i-i-i-itch** ...
**Stump!—scri-i-i-i-i-itch** ...

"Hugs are rosy-cozy," the bear went on in its whimsically winsome way. "Hugs make me feel fuzzy-wuzzy in my— GLAAAWWWRRKKK!!!!"

A moment later, Whimsy lay silenced on his side. Fluffy stuffy guts spilled from a slashy gash in his rum-tum-tummy, oozing onto the floor in a sorry-gory mess.

Elsewhere in the playroom, another toy broke into an inappropriately cheery song:

*"Floating along on a birthday cake*
*Upon a raspberry-soda-pop lake ...*

*Surrounded by choco-late sundae mountains,*
*Candy-cane rainbows and butter-scotch fountains . . . "*

It was Benny the Singing Dinosaur. Zombiekins turned and began walking stiffly toward the source of the music.

*"We'll merry-go-round the dreamy day long. . . ."* Benny sang.

**Stump!—scri-i-i-i-i-itch** ...

"*Singing our birthday-cake rowboat songs!*"

**Stump!—scri-i-i-i-i-itch** ...

"*Go for a swim with the iddle-bitty fishes* ..."

      **Stump!—scri-i-i-i-i-itch** ...

"*Tickling our toesies like Mummy's kisses—*"

There was a loud shower of sparks, and a severed dino head rolled away into a corner, where it went on singing like a broken record:

> "*Swim with the—fishes . . . Swim with the —fishes . . . Swim with the—fishes . . .*"

Zombiekins turned toward another corner of the playroom. . . .

"Schlemmo wants up," whimpered a furry orange toy far too adorable to be called a monster. Its voice was high-pitched and tinny, like some pre-adolescent chipmunk. "Up, up . . . Schlemmo wants up!"

Zombiekins started walking, stiffly and with a

limp, one leg dragging like a dead limb. . . .

**Stump!—scri-i-i-i-itch** . . .

"Schlemmo doesn't want to play right now," the cute and cuddly monster simpered.

**Stump!—scri-i-i-i-itch** . . .

"Up, up! Schlemmo wants up-up!" the toy too adorable to be called a monster begged in its tinny-tiny voice. But there was nobody to hear.

**Stump!—scri-i-i-i-itch** . . .

" . . . Schlemmo wants . . . Schlemmo doesn't—"

**THE NEXT MORNING, STANLEY WAS YANKED OUT**
of sleep bright and early by an alarm clock with no
snooze button—the cold wet nose of his dog Fetch.

"Nghhhh!" Stanley grumbled, rolling over. "Go
away.... Sleeping..."

But Fetch just climbed halfway onto Stanley's
bed, barking and licking Stanley's face.

"Bad dog!" Stanley drowsily protested. "Go!"

Fetch barked again and pointed out into the hall.

"Unghhh," Stanley groaned, wiping sleep from his eyes and dog slobber from his face. "Not *this* again."

Moments later, Fetch was dragging Stanley down the hall to the playroom once more. Stanley wasn't prepared for the grisly scene of toy-room tragedy he found there.

The floor was strewn with bits of savaged stuffies: Teddy bears with the stuffing ripped out of them ... Decapitated dinos ... A dismembered Schlemmo ...

Stanley just stood in the doorway, speechless.
At first he was too stunned to understand what had
happened. Then it started to sink in.

"Bad, Fetch!" Stanley scolded.

Boy, that dog had really done it this time. When
Stanley's mom found out about this, she was going
to send Fetch to a farm for sure, like she was always
threatening.

Stanley gave Fetch a dirty look. But instead of drooping his ears and tucking his tail between his legs in heartfelt canine remorse, the dumb dog just barked again and pointed to Zombiekins sitting unharmed in the middle of the crime scene.

Well, Stanley thought with relief, at least *his* toy had been spared. He took Zombiekins and put it in his school bag by the front door.

Then he went back to the playroom, gathered the remains of the other stuffies into a box, and hid them under his bed before he left for school. He didn't want Fetch to get sent to a farm. After all, the poor dog couldn't help it if he was born stupid.

**AT SCHOOL, ZOMBIEKINS WAS EVEN MORE OF A HIT** than Stanley could have hoped. Kids from all over the playground stopped whatever they were doing to crowd around him for a look at his weird, one-of-a-kind toy. Girls dropped their skipping ropes. Boys paused in the middle of pummeling each other. One kid wandered off the school grounds blindfolded when the friends he was playing blindfold tag with rushed away without telling him.

"Cool!" exclaimed Kathleen.

"Freaky!" complimented Fiona.

"Ew, gross!" squealed Butch.

"If you come anywhere near me with that thing," shrieked Big Tony, "I'll *scream!*"

But then a growl from the back of the crowd silenced all the others:

"Nice *doll*, Nudelman."

It was Knuckles Bruzkowski, the school bully.

The crowd around Stanley split up as quickly as it had formed. Girls hopscotched it out of there. Boys suddenly recalled they had people to punch at the other end of the yard. Somebody remembered the kid who was "it" in blindfold tag and went to retrieve him from traffic.

Knuckles was the terror of every kid in Dementedyville Elementary, but he always reserved a special place in his hurt for Stanley. He never saw Stanley without giving him a sucker punch, wedgie, or purple nurple—so when Stanley could help it, Knuckles never saw him at all.

But this time Stanley had let his guard down, and before he could duck for cover under the play structure, tunnel though the sand to safety, run home and transfer to another school, Knuckles grabbed hold of him.

And the next thing Stanley knew, he was dangling upside down in the chains of the tire swing and Knuckles was clenching Zombiekins in one of his meaty fists.

"Why are its eyes like that?" Knuckles grunted, holding the strange stuffy away from him as if he wasn't sure what to make of it.

"I-I got it at Mrs. Imavitch's yard sale," Stanley stammered.

Knuckles' eyes widened.

"You got this from *the Widow*?" he said. Stanley would've almost said he looked afraid.

The bell rang. All over the school ground, children stopped laughing and playing and trudged into line like condemned prisoners. Stanley felt a wave of panic, remembering the time Knuckles hung him from the basketball net at first recess on a rainy day and he wasn't discovered until home time. (His teeth still chattered just thinking about it.)

"Hey," said a voice behind them. "Give that back to Stanley right now!"

It was Miranda, of course. She was the only kid in school who ever dared stand up to Knuckles.

Knuckles' lips curled in a snarl, but he didn't make a move toward her.

47

Instead he just wrenched the swing tighter around Stanley.

"*Make me*," Knuckles growled.

"We're not afraid of you, Duane," Miranda said.

Knuckles' eyes flashed with anger at the mention of his given name. He cranked the swing another couple notches.

"Yes, we are!" Stanley squeaked.

Fortunately, at that moment, the duty teacher Mrs. Plumdotty saw them from across the yard.

"*Stan*-ley," she called from the back door, where she was herding kids into the school. "Stop playing on those swings and line up. You heard the bell, dear."

"Yeah, Stanley, dear," Knuckles snorted. He gave Zombiekins one last, uncertain look and stuffed it into the space where the chain made a collar around Stanley's neck. Then he wound the swing a couple notches tighter and released it with a spin.

"*Catch you later*, Nudelman," Knuckles growled as he lumbered away.

**ALL THE WAY UP TO THEIR CLASS ON THE THIRD**
floor, Stanley had to listen to Miranda lecture
him for the hundredth time about standing up to
Knuckles. She had this theory that Knuckles would
leave Stanley alone if only he would stick up for
himself. Stanley had his own theory—that whenever Miranda did stick up for him, it only made
Knuckles' poundings worse.

Halfway up the last flight of stairs, they were startled by a voice from above.

"*Mister* Nudelman..."

Their teacher Mr. Baldengrumpy was standing at the top of the stairwell with a look on his face like he'd just bitten into a pickled lemon.

Stanley froze. It was never good when a teacher called you "Mister."

"Did you *really* expect to get away with it this time?" Mr. Baldengrumpy croaked.

It didn't take Stanley long to guess what his teacher was cross about. Mr. Baldengrumpy was obsessed with walking properly in lines. He made the class practice fire drills three times a week. Three times a week he marched them up and down the halls, teaching them to be quiet by yelling at them. He said they had to learn to exit the building in a slow and orderly manner in case there was ever a real fire. If there was ever a real fire, he wanted to be sure his class could exit the slowest.

One of Mr. Baldengrumpy's rules was that they had to walk up the stairs on the left, down on the right. Stanley didn't mean to be a troublemaker, but he was always forgetting.

"Well, you can just march back down there and come up again on the right side," Mr. Baldengrumpy barked.

"Er, but I thought you said we were supposed to come up on the *left*?" Stanley meekly replied.

"*Don't get smart with me, young man!*" Mr. Baldengrumpy fumed.

So Stanley trudged all the way back down the stairs and came up again on the right side, which is to say, the left.

In class, Stanley was in trouble again before he could even take his book out for the first lesson. He was just minding his own business while the rest of the class copied out some spelling words when for no reason at all Felicity Lickspittle piped up from the desk in front of him, "Mr. Baldengrumpy, Stanley has a *toy* in his desk."

Mr. Baldengrumpy stopped writing on the chalkboard and glared down at Stanley, whose first reflex was naturally to shove Zombiekins deeper into his desk. But that only made his teacher more cross.

Stanley handed Zombiekins over and Mr. Baldengrumpy set it on a table at the front with a sniff of disgust.

"Now *don't* interrupt my lesson again, young man," he warned.

Stanley wanted to point out that he wasn't the one who interrupted in the first place—that actually he had done his best to cover things up so they could all carry on with the lesson like nothing happened. But something about the look on Mr. Baldengrumpy's face told him there was no point splitting hairs.

As soon as Mr. Baldengrumpy turned back to the chalkboard, Felicity looked around and stuck her tongue out at Stanley.

9

**IT WAS A LITTLE WHILE LATER THAT STANLEY'S**
school day *really* took a turn for the worse.

The trouble started halfway through first period,
when Mr. Baldengrumpy brought out a projector. The
class cheered. They were going to watch a movie!

Mr. Baldengrumpy explained he had a science film for them called *Our Neighbor, the Moon*.

The class groaned. Did he have to ruin *everything* by making it so "educational"?

But Mr. Baldengrumpy just started the film anyway and sat down at his desk to pretend to mark homework. Within minutes he had dozed off behind a stack of books and the whole class was educated half out of their minds.

"If I was any more educated, I'd be in a coma," grumbled Fiona. "Why do we have to watch this?"

"This is the lamest space movie ever," griped Kathleen. "When are they gonna blow something up with lasers?"

"Shhhh!!!" hissed Felicity, hunched over a notebook taking color-coded notes.

Stanley, meanwhile, was doing his best to pay attention to the movie because he didn't want to get in any more trouble with his teacher.

So nobody noticed when the small stuffy on the edge of the front desk, illuminated by an image of the full moon, twitched one floppy bunny ear and shivered like someone stirring from sleep....

Slowly, one of its eyes blinked open, gazing straight ahead with a cold blank stare....

Stanley was finding it hard to concentrate on the film. Normally he loved space movies, but this one was seriously lacking in the freaky-aliens-with-death-rays department. It was just a lot of boring moon footage with a voice droning out such fascinating facts as how many paper cups you would have to stack one on top of the other to reach the moon.

Stanley wondered how they figured that out. He imagined a team of space scientists stacking paper cups day after day. They would've needed really tall ladders.

Suddenly, though, a shriek from the desk in front of him shattered his concentration.

"Mr. Baldengrumpy!" Felicity wailed. "Stanley's doll just *bit* me!"

**MR. BALDENGRUMPY STOPPED THE MOVIE. SOME-**
body flicked on the lights.

Zombiekins was sitting motionless on the edge
of the front desk. Just a harmless stuffy, albeit with a
somewhat macabre, half-dead appearance. But Felicity shrank from it in terror, holding her math book in
front of her like a shield.

"I-it bit me right here," she claimed, pointing to a spot on the back of her wrist.

There wasn't a mark, as far as Stanley could see, but naturally Mr. Baldengrumpy believed her anyway.

SPUTTER CLOSE UP

"I suppose this is your idea of a joke?" Mr. Baldengrumpy sputtered. Sputtered means he said it in an angry voice and emphasized his point by showering Stanley with spit droplets.

"I-I didn't—" Stanley stammered. "I-I never—"

But Mr. Baldengrumpy wasn't even listening. He just carried Zombiekins to his desk at the back of the room, muttering something about how he "should've gone to law school like Mother wanted." Then he told the class to take out their math books.

"Aw, what about the rest of the movie?" moaned Fiona.

"Now we'll never know how it turns out," groaned Kathleen.

But Mr. Baldengrumpy was always cranky when he didn't get his nap. He assigned the class three pages of word problems and the children moaned in agony—which seemed to cheer him up a bit.

From across the room, Miranda gave Stanley a questioning look. What was going on?

Stanley shrugged, then pointed at Felicity and made the crazy sign with his finger. Obviously she was making the whole thing up. There was no way Zombiekins could've actually bitten her.

Was there?

Stanley remembered the Widow's mysterious warnings ("*Zat is no ordinary toy....*") and turned to look back at his teacher's desk....

But Zombiekins had disappeared!

Quickly, Stanley pushed his pencil off the edge of his desk and bent down to pick it up—just in time to see Zombiekins shuffling out of the classroom through the hall door....

**STANLEY STOOD UP AND SIDLED**
over to the pencil sharpener by the
front door, counting on his fingers
in his best impersonation of a boy
embroiled in a math problem. He waited
until Mr. Baldengrumpy wasn't looking, then snatched a bathroom pass and
slipped out into the hall.

He didn't see Zombiekins, so
he ducked into the nearest cubby and crouched
behind some coats.

Once he was sure he wasn't being
watched, he darted from his cover—dove—
rolled—scrambled to his feet
in another cubby across the

hall—and pressed himself against the wall to catch his breath.

Then, from hiding place to hiding place, he zigged, zagged, crept, crawled, slipped, slunk, tumbled,stumbled, hopped (stubbed toe), and vaulted down the hall, moving like a cat. Like an extremely paranoid cat. He swooped, shimmied, slithered on his elbows, pounced, prowled, paused to wipe a mashed-banana stain from his shirtfront, hunched, hurdled, wriggled, wormed, tiptoed, leapfrogged, somersaulted, sprang, and—

BONK!ed his head on a lunch box straightening up.

Why was Stanley being so sneaky?

No reason. This was just how he always went to the bathroom

at school. You should've seen him fetch the attendance register.

He was crawling on his hands and knees across the floor, concealed under a yellow raincoat to avoid attracting suspicion, when the door to the grade 6 class opened. Thinking quickly, Stanley jumped to his feet and disguised himself as part of a display project on Egypt.

He held his breath as the sixth graders filed past on their way to the library.

Last in line was Knuckles. He slouched by without giving Stanley a second glance. But halfway down the hall he stopped and sniffed the air like a jungle cat scenting its prey.

Stanley thought for sure he'd been discovered. But Knuckles just grunted, shook his head, and lumbered ahead to catch up with his class.

When the sixth graders had gone, Stanley searched their empty classroom ... the rest of the hall ... the boys' bathroom. . . .

But there was no trace of Zombiekins anywhere.

Stanley was baffled. It was as if Zombiekins had just vanished. The rest of the classroom doors were closed, and he'd checked everywhere else it could possibly...

Unless...

*No...*

Stanley tried to push the thought from his mind. It was too, too awful.

*Not that...Anything but that...*

**A MOMENT LATER, STANLEY FOUND HIMSELF**
sneaking into the girl's bathroom. He kept his eyes
trained on the floor and shaded
them with one hand so
he wouldn't accidentally
glimpse anything too
psychologically damag-
ing. He knew he must be
surrounded by millions of
tiny girl germs and made a note to decontaminate
himself at recess by rolling in some dirt.

But it wasn't long before Stanley's curiosity
started to get the better of him and he peeked around
between a couple fingers....

Stanley had always expected it would be like his Mom's bathroom at home—little flower-shaped soaps you weren't supposed to use, frilly towels that were only for show, that thick perfumey smell that always made him sneeze....

But actually it was a lot like the boys' bathroom. He started to relax a little.

And that's when the door to the hall swung open behind him!

Stanley spun around in a flood of embarrassment —which quickly turned to terror—

For there, standing in the doorway, was Knuckles!

"I thought I smelt you sneaking around in here," Knuckles grunted. "Weirdo."

"I-I was just looking for something. . . ." Stanley stammered.

Knuckles took two menacing steps toward Stanley and the door closed behind him. The noise it made in the echoey bathroom was like the stone door to a tomb slamming shut.

"You shouldn't be in here, Nudelman," he sneered, coming closer. "What if something bad was to happen to you? Ha, ha. . . ."

Stanley backed away in terror, cursing himself for letting Knuckles catch him off guard twice in the same day. But before Stanley could slip past Knuckles by creating a diversion, flee the building, change his name and move to Australia, Knuckles grabbed hold of him again.

And the next thing Stanley knew, his head was wedged under Knuckles' armpit and he was staring down into a gleaming white toilet bowl.

"You know," Knuckles said in a reflective tone, "I almost feel bad about this. . . ."

"R-r-really?" Stanley squeaked, a faint hope stirring inside him.

"Naw," Knuckles sneered, pushing Stanley forward.

What happened next was all a blur. One moment Stanley was staring helplessly down at his own terrified reflection getting larger and larger…

Then a weird noise rang in his ears:

**Stump!—scri-i-i-i-itch**…

Knuckles stood up, yanking Stanley back. They both froze, listening. The noise echoed around the room like a rubber ball bouncing off all the walls. When it finally died out, they heard it again. Only this time it was closer:

**Stump!—scri-i-i-i-i-itch**...

Whatever was making the strange noise was in the next stall over—and sounded like it was dragging itself toward them!

Then they saw it....

**Stump!—scri-i-i-i-i-itch**...

From under the partition between the stalls it came...Staggering slowly toward them...Moving stiffly, with a pronounced limp....

It was...

73

**Zombiekins!!!**

Obviously.

Like, *duh*.

Still, it was a shock. Even Stanley found the sight of it a little unsettling: The cold, dead eyes . . . the fierce, sharp fangs . . . the one floppy bunny ear. . . .

"Hey, isn't that your *doll*?" Knuckles snorted in a mocking tone—but Stanley heard a nervous tremor in his voice too. "Why's it following us like that?"

Knuckles backed out of the stall, dragging Stanley with him. Zombiekins just turned sharply and continued lurching in their direction.

"I-I don't know," Stanley replied. "I never even realized it was battery-powered."

Soon they were backed up against a wall and Knuckles was holding Stanley in front of him like a shield. Still Zombiekins kept coming.

"Make it stop, Nudelman," Knuckles whimpered. "Seriously, or else I'll—hunh?!"

Zombiekins latched onto Knuckles' pant leg.

"Get it off me!" Knuckles screamed, sliding down the wall. "Get it—AAAHHHHHHH!!!"

As Knuckles crumpled to the floor, his grip loosened and Stanley was able to break free and step away. . . .

Knuckles' eyes bulged and his mouth gaped open, but the only sound that came out was a sort of strangled gurgling—as if he was too choked with terror to scream.

For a moment, Stanley stood frozen in shock. Then, coming to his senses, he turned and bolted for the door. Behind him, the bathroom echoed with piteous smacking, smooching, puckering noises....

Stanley broke out into the hall just as Knuckles suddenly found his voice:

**STANLEY BURST INTO HIS CLASSROOM. HIS HEART** was pounding. His breath came in great heaving gulps. His head was spinning with everything he'd just seen....

But his classmates were just working quietly at their desks. Nobody even noticed him come in.

"... Agahgahgrrraaghagahgrraaghllhh ..."
Knuckles' wail echoed through the hall behind him.

Stanley started to slam the door, then caught himself and shut it carefully, with a tiny click.

Mr. Baldengrumpy looked up from his desk at the back.

Knuckles' screams went on and on, muffled only slightly by the door.

"...agahgahgahgahgahgahg ..."

Mr. Baldengrumpy gave Stanley a narrow look.

"You weren't *running in the halls* just now, were you?" he asked accusingly.

"N-no, sir," Stanley panted.

"I hope not," Mr. Baldengrumpy replied, in a voice like he didn't for one minute believe it. "Because you know we don't run in the halls."

Stanley waited for him to say more, but Mr. Baldengrumpy just went back to writing F's on the students' art assignments.

So Stanley went and sat down at his desk.

"*Mrmmrngmrmarnnnnn...*" Felicity mumbled to herself in front of him. Stanley couldn't make out what she was saying and didn't bother to ask. He had way too much running through his mind.

Somebody should check to make sure Knuckles was all right, Stanley thought. For a moment he considered telling his teacher what had happened....

"*Mrmmrngmrmarnnnnn...*"

No, obviously he wasn't thinking clearly. Mr. Baldengrumpy would never believe him. And even if he did, he'd only find some way to blame it all on Stanley.

"*Mrmmrngmrmarnnnnn...*"

Anyway, Zombiekins was just a toy. Surely it wouldn't actually *hurt* Knuckles.

But there was definitely *something* weird going on here. Stanley decided to talk to Miranda about it at recess. She always knew what to do.

As soon as he had made up his mind, Stanley felt a lot calmer and he was able to focus on pretending to do his work again.

"*Mrmmrngmrmarnnnnn...*"

Except now Stanley noticed for the first time that Felicity had been moaning to herself ever since he sat down. Stanley jabbed her in the shoulder with his pencil stub.

"Hey," he whispered. "Keep it down."

Felicity started turning around to face him. But her movements were weirdly stiff and slow, and her shoulders didn't turn at all. Her head just swiveled around, inch by inch, with a noise like an old gate creaking....

She was so changed Stanley hardly recognized her: Her eyes were clouded over like gray marbles. Her skin was the color of clam chowder. Her hairstyle was askew.

"Are you all right?" Stanley asked in shock.

He could tell there was something seriously wrong with her. Felicity would *never* let her hair get like that.

But she didn't answer him. She just moaned again and slowly, as if it took enormous effort, reached one hand up—

—and grabbed Stanley by the throat!

"Hey—" Stanley gasped, choking out the words. "—are you—crazy?!"

But Felicity just stared right through him with blank, clouded-over eyes.

"All right class," Mr. Baldengrumpy announced in a bored tone from his desk at the back, "put away your books and get ready for recess."

Kids sprang out of their seats, leaped into the aisles, danced, pranced, romped and gamboled to get their things and line up. Felicity lifted Stanley up out of his chair by the neck and shook him.

Sophia frolicked out to the hall to get her coat. Lydia skipped into line at the door. Jack twirled into the hall on his tippy-toes. Big Tony bounded to the front of the class to get a skipping rope from the box of recess toys. Fiona and Kathleen pushed and shoved to grab the hardest bouncy ball to use for murderball. Felicity bashed Stanley's head against his desk like she was trying to crack open a coconut.

WHAM
WHAM
WHAM

"Stanley Nudelman," Mr. Baldengrumpy barked impatiently from the back. "Stop fooling around and get ready for recess."

Stanley tried to call to him for help, but all that came out was "Gack!" and "Hlp!"

"And don't *mumble*," Mr. Baldengrumpy scolded. "You really must learn to speak up."

Stanley couldn't breathe. . . . He felt himself starting to black out. . . .

But then the bell rang. As soon as it did, Felicity dropped Stanley to the floor and started lurching obediently out to recess.

Stanley lay on the floor, gasping and rubbing his throat.

"Hurry up, Stanley," Mr. Baldengrumpy said gruffly. "You'll never amount to anything in this world until you learn to walk quietly in a straight line with everybody else."

**14**

**"I'M TELLING YOU, SHE'S A ZOMBIE."**

"Stanley," said Miranda, "you've always had a pretty wild imagination, but this time you've finally gone nuts. Zombies only exist in the movies."

"Oh, yeah?" Stanley said. "Look at her. That's all she's been doing all recess."

Normally Felicity liked to spend her recesses holding the duty teacher's hand and tattling on kids who were breaking nitpicky safety rules like no climbing fences, no running up the slide, and no using the teeter-totter as a human catapult.

"She's just being stuck up," Miranda said.

"Okay, so what about Knuckles?" Stanley asked. "You should've heard him screaming."

Stanley shuddered just remembering it.

"That only proves what I've been telling you all along—that he's really just a big chicken baby," Miranda said. "Look, Stanley, Zombiekins is just a toy. There's no way it could actually hurt kids."

"I know what I saw," Stanley insisted. "There, look at her now—"

Felicity was lurching out onto the soccer pitch.

"So? Maybe she wants to play soccer."

"And risk getting a speck of dirt on her pretty, pretty dress?" Stanley said. "You know how she feels about 'perspiring.'"

"Okay, so maybe she is acting a little weird," Miranda admitted. "But that still doesn't make her a zombie."

Someone booted the soccer ball and it drilled Felicity in the side of the head. She didn't even flinch.

The kids stopped playing soccer and crowded around Felicity to ask if she was all right. But she just stood there, swaying slightly, without replying. Then she stooped over, picked up the soccer ball, and held it out in front of her as if she'd never seen anything like it before.

"See?" Stanley said. Even Miranda was starting to look doubtful.

Once the kids around Felicity realized she was okay, they started bugging her to give the ball back so they could get on with their game.

But Felicity just opened her mouth wide . . . and shoved the ball in!

**FINALLY MIRANDA BELIEVED STANLEY.**

"You keep Felicity out of trouble," she told him on the way up to class. "And I'll go check the girls' bathroom for Zombiekins and Knuckles."

"What do you mean, 'Keep her out of trouble?'" Stanley said, looking over his shoulder in alarm. "She wants to *eat* me."

Felicity was five places behind Stanley in line. When he turned to look back, she snarled, gnashed her teeth, and stretched a clutching hand out toward him. But fortunately she wouldn't leave her place in line to get him.

"Stanley," Miranda said, lowering her voice confidentially, "do you have any idea how much trouble you'll be in if Mr. Baldengrumpy finds out *your toy* turned her into a zombie? You've got to keep her from doing anything to draw attention to her, uh, *condition*."

And with that, Miranda ducked out of line and hurried up the stairs.

Just ahead of Stanley, Fiona was dangling a worm in Big Tony's face.

"Ewwww!" screamed Big Tony. "Get it away from me!"

Fiona giggled and, with Kathleen egging her on, flung the worm at Big Tony. It stuck to the front of his shirt. He let out a piercing shriek, then danced and squirmed and slapped at his clothes like someone on fire until the worm finally shook loose and dropped onto the stair.

Fiona and Kathleen doubled over laughing. The rest of the line just kept trudging up the stairs.

Except Felicity. When she came to the worm, she stopped and pounced on it.... She rose up, holding it out in front of her...then popped it into her mouth and swallowed!

The line stopped and the noisy stairwell fell silent. Everyone stared at Felicity. Big Tony put his hand over his mouth like he was going to be sick.

It was a tense moment. Stanley knew he had to do

something to cover up before his classmates started to get suspicious.

"Uh, three-second rule?" he shrugged.

The other kids looked at him as if he was mental. Except for Fiona and Kathleen, who just nodded their heads and stared at Felicity with surprised admiration.

"Cool," said Kathleen.

16

**ONCE THEY REACHED THE TOP FLOOR, THE LINE**
broke up, and kids scattered off in all directions to
their cubbies. Felicity came shuffling after Stanley,
lurching slowly and stiffly like... well, like a zombie....

He barely had time to dig his homework out of his knapsack, check that his mom had signed it, change into his indoor shoes, tie them in double knots, zip up his bag, open it again to grab a pencil from his pencil case, close it again, and narrowly escape before Felicity reached him.

Stanley took his seat inside the classroom and Felicity came staggering straight toward him, barging between the desks instead of taking the aisles. That's when Stanley realized he had a BIG problem: No matter how slow-moving Felicity was, as long as he stayed put she'd eventually catch him. But he couldn't run away without getting in trouble for being out of his desk.

Felicity kept lumbering in his direction . . . gnashing her teeth . . . clawing the air. . . .

Soon she was just a few lurches away. . . .

Stanley weighed his options: Mauled by a zombie? Or yelled at by his teacher?

He shrunk down as small as he could make himself at his desk. He decided he was more afraid of Mr. Baldengrumpy.

The next moment, Felicity was hovering right over him and Stanley was leaning way, way back to avoid the clutching hands that stretched . . . toward . . . his . . . neck. . . .

"Okay, class," Mr. Baldengrumpy droned. "Take your seats."

Felicity stopped and stiffened; her grip was cold as stone around Stanley's throat.

She unclenched his neck, shuffled ahead, and thumped down in her chair. As soon as she was seated, she swiveled her head around to hiss and bare her teeth at Stanley.

"Who would like to hand out the books?" Mr. Baldengrumpy asked.

Felicity's head swiveled to the front again. Her arm shot into the air, stiff and grasping, like a hand reaching up out of a freshly dug grave.

"*Mrmmrngmrmarnnnnn*..." she moaned loudly.

"Thank you, Felicity," said Mr. Baldengrumpy, setting the books down on her desk.

**ELSEWHERE IN THE SCHOOL, IT WAS CENTER TIME** downstairs in Ms. Mellow's kindergarten and the classroom was bustling with non-gender-specific role-playing activities. Little girls in red firefighter hats were tearing around making siren noises, filling buckets at the Water Station and splashing them on a pretend fire at the Computer Station. Little boys were at the Craft Table, eating crayons and glue. In the Playhouse, one boy was pretending to be the kind of daddy who liked to wear an apron and bake mud pies, while the girl he was playing with was pretending to be the kind of mommy who liked to throw dishes and yell at you to get a job.

And in the middle of the busy room, one child stood all by himself, picking his nose with intense concentration.

In the sandbox, a little girl with pigtails was trying to soothe a little boy who was crying. He was crying because she'd just whacked him over the head with her plastic spade.

"There, there," said the little girl with pigtails, patting the boy on the shoulder. And when that didn't work, she dumped a pail of sand on him.

Over in the Story Corner, two boys who both wanted to read the same book were having a tug-of-war.

"Now, boys," Ms. Mellow chimed in a soothing singsong. "Remember, we always *share*."

Ms. Mellow's voice was so calm and sweet, it worked on the children like a spell: As soon as they heard her, the two boys stopped fighting and put the book scraps down on the floor where they could both read them together, with all the words and pictures upside down. And the kid who was picking his nose stopped and offered some to a girl who was bashing toy trucks together nearby.

At the back of the room, a small boy with glasses was playing by himself in the Doll Corner. Little Georgie liked to play with dolls, and there was nothing wrong with that. He liked to talk to himself in different voices and pretend it was the dolls talking, and there was nothing wrong with that. He liked to make the dolls scream in terror and rip each other limb from limb in a murderous rampage with the gnawing and the clawing and the gnashing and the smashing. . . .

And there was nothing wrong that.

Little Georgie was piling all the dollhouse furniture into barricades when he noticed a strange new toy staggering toward him from out of the coatroom.

It was some sort of stuffy, like a cross between a teddy bear and a stuffed bunny. Except it had fangs like the pointy bit on an electric can opener, claws as sharp as fishhooks, and something unnerving about its eyes.

"Ooo," Little Georgie exclaimed. "Cute."

Little Georgie picked up the weird toy. But as he cradled it in his arms, it wriggled and stretched its mouth toward his neck. ...

"Aaaaaah!!!" Little Georgie squealed. "Nooooooooooo!!!"

Suddenly the Doll Corner rang with loud, piteous smackings and smoochings.

"Oo—ahh—STOP—ughh!!!" Little Georgie choked. "THAT—oo—ahh—arr—TICKLES—urrff!!!!"

A few minutes later, the little girl with pigtails got bored of burying the little crying boy in sand and came to see what Georgie was doing in the dollhouse.

"That doesn't go there," she said, lifting a sofa from one of Georgie's barricades. "It goes *here*."

She started removing all the furniture from Georgie's piles and placing it in the dollhouse rooms.

"And this goes here. ... And this goes here . . . . " she said in a bossy tone.

"*Hmmgrgh…*" whimpered Georgie. He was hunched over, biting the head off a doll in a tuxedo.

"*I* want that," the little girl in pigtails said. She grabbed at Georgie's doll.

"*Mgnhrgnhhh*," Georgie moaned, hugging it to his chest.

"*Give* it," the girl said. "You already had a turn."

She yanked and yanked until finally Georgie snapped at her, sinking his teeth into her wrist!

"Ow! I'm telling!" she threatened. "Ms. Mellow says you have to share, it's the–oo, I feel straaaaaange. . . ."

The little girl with pigtails put her hand to her head. Her face turned gray. A dull, clouded-over look came into her eyes.

"I think I'm going to *hmmnrhghghrghgh* …"

PA-TOOIE!

**UPSTAIRS, MEANWHILE, FELICITY KEPT MAKING**
hungry noises in Stanley's direction, but luckily she
wouldn't leave her desk unless Mr. Baldengrumpy
gave her permission.

Still, Stanley was afraid his teacher would
notice something was wrong with her. Every time
Mr. Baldengrumpy asked for volunteers to collect
work or do chores around the room, she whimpered
like a begging dog. And she bellowed with enthusi-
asm whenever he cracked a corny joke.

So in other words she was pretty much her usual
self.

Except that her "work" was nothing but scribbles
and at one point while washing the blackboard she
chugalugged a box of chalk. Fortunately nobody

noticed except Fiona and Kathleen, who just nodded in appreciation.

"Sick," Fiona complimented.

"Nasty," Kathleen praised.

When Miranda came back from checking the girls' bathroom, she gave Stanley a shrug from the door to let him know her search had come up empty. But they didn't get a chance to talk until halfway through the period, when on a secret signal they met at the pencil sharpener.

"The bathroom was empty," Miranda whispered. "So I searched the rest of the floor again—but there was no trace of Zombiekins anywhere."

"What about Knuckles?" Stanley asked with concern. "Was he with his class?"

"I don't know," Miranda shrugged. "The door to the sixth graders' room was closed."

"Something terrible has happened to him," Stanley said. "I just know it."

"Calm down, Stanley," Miranda said. "We don't know for sure that anything happened to Knuckles. So for now, let's just worry about keeping Felicity out of trouble. . . .

". . . and finding Zombiekins before anyone else does. . . . "

**MEANWHILE, DOWN IN THE SCHOOL'S BASEMENT,**
the hall was filled with the sound of cats drowning to
the tune of "Old MacDonald."

Mrs. Bernstein, the music teacher, was conduct-
ing the third graders. She stood at the front of the
Music Room waving a conductor's baton with her
eyes closed like someone in a trance.

To one side of the room, the string section was choking the cellos, battering the bass viols and doing violence to the violins. Across from them, the horn section was blaring like a traffic jam of angry cab drivers.

"Beautiful, boys and girls," Mrs. Bernstein beamed. "Marvelous!"

Underneath all this racket throbbed the dull haunting drone of Bubba on the tuba, who didn't know the tune and was blundering along with a noise like a ship lost in fog.

The kids all seemed to be enjoying themselves, especially Delores, who was doing air guitar moves on the ukulele, strutting and jiving and windmilling her strumming hand without really playing anything.

"Lovely, Delores!" Mrs. Bernstein cooed.

Mrs. Bernstein raised her baton to signal the finale was coming, then brought it down with a sharp flick. The tune tumbled to a halt with everyone finishing at different times and on different parts. Mrs. Bernstein clapped her hands together in delight.

"Bravo, everyone!" she sang. "That was fabulous!

"Okay," Mrs. Bernstein trilled, "let's try it again with a Latin feel. . . . "

"Aw, can't we play 'Three Blind Mice'?" whined Jason.

"Pardon me, Jason?" Mrs. Bernstein smiled, removing a plug from her left ear.

"Why do we always have to play 'Old MacDonald'?" Jason complained. "Why can't we ever play 'Three Blind Mice'?"

"Or 'Hot Cross Buns'?" said Alycha.

"I wanna play 'Smoke on the Water'. . . . "

"How about 'Ride of the Valkyries'?"

"All right, children," Mrs. Bernstein smiled, replacing her earplug. "You may all play whatever you like." She tapped her baton on the music stand. "On three . . ."

All the kids played their hearts out. Except for a girl named Mackenzie in the back row of the horn section. She had stopped playing momentarily to watch how the boy beside her produced such a wonderful tone from his trumpet—as if he'd trapped some strange animal inside that was screaming to get out.

That's why she was the only one who noticed when a strange stuffy appeared from behind a pile of violin cases by the door. It was small and creepy-cute and it moved on its own like something alive—or at least like something not quite dead.

Mackenzie watched, mesmerized, as the weird stuffy dragged itself along the floor, weaving through tapping feet, chair legs and music stands. It seemed to be heading straight for her, and as it got closer, she heard a faint noise under the racket of her classmates' playing:

**Stump!—scri-i-i-i-i-itch** ... **Stump!—scri-i-i-i-i-itch** ... **Stump!—scri-i-i-i-i-itch** ...

Soon the creepy-cute bunny monster had crossed the room. When it was almost at Mackenzie's feet, she bent down to pick it up. ...

**SHORTLY BEFORE LUNCH, STANLEY SLIPPED OUT OF**
class to search the school again while Miranda stayed
behind to watch Felicity.

He didn't find Zombiekins, but he did run into
Knuckles' class down in the gym. He knew it was
them by the horrible noises spilling out into the hall,
like the sounds from some medieval torture chamber: Howls of pain . . . Shrieks of terror . . . Loud whaps
of slapping flesh . . .

They were playing dodgeball.

Personally, Stanley hated dodgeball. He didn't
approve of games that involved targeting children
with dangerous projectiles. At least, he didn't approve
of games that involved targeting *him* with dangerous
projectiles. But Stanley's gym teacher Mr. Straap said

dodgeball was "character building" and made his class play it at least once a week.

Stanley halted outside the gym, listening to the horrifying racket: Foul curses and bitter threats. Battle whoops and warlike grunts. Desperate pleas and demonic laughter.

Obviously the sixth graders were enjoying themselves.

Stanley snuck onto the gym stage through the side entrance and hid behind a stack of gymnastic mats. It was the sixth graders, all right. The gym was a seething battlefield. Stanley winced as he watched one boy take a ball in the face from point-blank range.

"Owww!" the boy wailed, pinching his nostrils to stem the dripping blood. "I tink my doze id boken!"

"Walk it off, Toppleover," said Mr. Straap. "You're holding up the game."

But Knuckles was nowhere to be seen.

Stanley knew then that something awful must have happened to him. Knuckles wouldn't have missed dodgeball for *anything*.

Stanley slipped out into the hall again and was on his way back to class when something caught his eye. Around the corner from the gym was the Science Closet, where they stored stuff for science classes. Normally the room was kept locked at all times because teachers didn't want children getting into things and learning about science without supervision. But now Stanley noticed the door was open a crack. . . .

He gave the door a tiny, cautious push. . . .

It swung open with an eerie *creeeeeeak*—they always do—and Stanley took a deep breath and stepped inside. . . .

The room was windowless and dark, and the junk scattered on the floor and crammed onto shelves cast weird shadows on all the walls. Stanley took a few steps in—then jumped back when he felt a cobweb brush against his face. . . .

Fortunately, it turned out to be just a butterfly net hanging from a shelf.

Unfortunately, when Stanley jumped back he got tangled in a *real* cobweb. He thought he felt something large and hairy crawling down the back of his shirt. . . .

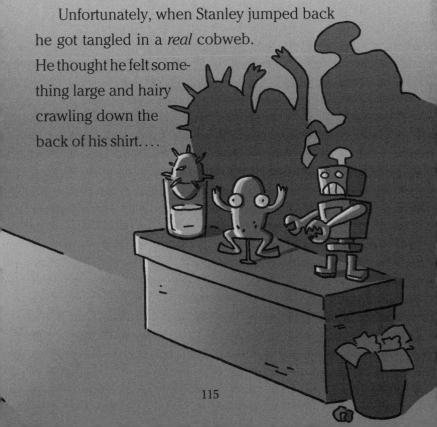

Stanley stood in the middle of the room, too afraid to move. All this spooky description was creeping him out. Then he thought he heard something...

*Da-dum...da-dum...da-dum...*

A steady thumping, like the music before something really bad happens in a scary movie...Stanley froze, listening as hard as he could....

*Da-dum...da-dum...da-dum...*

He couldn't tell where it was coming from, but it was definitely getting louder—and faster!

**Da-dum—da-dum—da-dum—**

Stanley felt a surge of terror—and the ominous music accelerated!

**Dadum-dadum-dadum-dadum—**

He wanted to scream but he was struck dumb with terror. The noise just kept building and building.... He didn't know which way to turn or where to run.... It seemed to be coming from right under—

Oh. Right.

Stanley put his hand on his chest.

It was just his heart beating.

He relaxed a little and the thumping quickly subsided.

But still, he was so creeped out he decided to get

out of there. He turned to go—and that's when he saw it!

Stanley felt woozy and had to lean up against the wall.

Oh, poor Knuckles! No matter how rotten he was, he didn't deserve this!

Stanley was flooded with memories of all the things he would've missed out on if it weren't for Knuckles: The recesses spent buried upside down in snowbanks. The nights padlocked to the bicycle rack.

The time he slalomed face-first down three flights of stairs lashed to a skateboard with skipping ropes. (Kids *still* talked about that.)

And now, after all they had shared together, *his* toy had done this to Knuckles. Stanley felt like he was going to be sick. . . .

But suddenly a jolt of terror brought him to his senses. He had to get out of there, and fast—before the same thing happened to him!

He turned to flee—but the door creaked open behind him with a blinding flash that froze him to the spot!

**"THERE YOU ARE. I'VE BEEN LOOKING ALL OVER** for you."

When Stanley's eyes blinked back into focus, Miranda was standing in the doorway with her hand on the light switch.

"Don't come in!" he warned her. "Run! Save yourself!"

"What are you talking about?" Miranda asked.

"Look. . ." Stanley said, pointing to the gaping cadaver in the corner. But he couldn't bear to look himself.

"Yeah, so?" Miranda said. "What's the big deal?"

"WHAT'S THE BIG DEAL?!?" Stanley gasped. "How can you SAY such a thing? I mean, I know you never liked him, but—"

"What are you talking about?" Miranda asked.

"*What am I talking about?*" Stanley shouted. He never expected Miranda could be so coldhearted. "Just *look* at him!"

That's when he happened to sneak a peek over his shoulder himself....

Oops.

It wasn't Knuckles after all. It was only Cross-Section Guy from Health Class.

Stanley felt pretty foolish.

"Er, yeahhhhhh, just look at him," he repeated, trying to cover up his mistake. "I mean, look what somebody did to his vitals."

Cross-Section Guy had a brain jammed into his stomach cavity, a clump of intestines spilling out of his skull, and a balled-up pair of old gym socks where his heart should've been.

"Whatever," Miranda said, like she wasn't going to waste her time arguing with a nutcase. "Hurry up. We better check on Felicity."

Miranda tossed him his backpack—typically she had thought to bring it along—and together they headed for the school cafeteria.

"What were you crawling around in the dark for anyway?" Miranda asked as they weaved through the lunchtime crowds.

"Um, no reason," Stanley mumbled.

**THE LUNCHROOM WAS FULL BY THE TIME STANLEY** and Miranda arrived, but they had no trouble finding Felicity. She was sitting in front of a huge mound of food and a crowd of classmates were gathered around, watching her stuff one sandwich from the pile after another into her mouth: bologna, egg salad, peanut butter and jam, liverwurst and grape jelly....

Kathleen and Fiona kept bringing more food and Felicity kept wolfing it down. She leaned forward and gobbled a tray of cold french fries without using her hands, like a pig rooting in a trough. She crunched and swallowed a turkey leg, bones and all. She tipped back a carton of coffee creamer and emptied it in a few gulps. Then she ate the carton.

Stanley and Miranda sat at a corner table by themselves. But when Stanley went to take out his lunch, there was nothing in his bag except the Widow's taffy. He had been so busy disposing of the evidence of Fetch's crime spree that morning, he must have forgotten to pack a lunch.

"Great," Stanley muttered. "First I accidentally turn Felicity into a zombie, now *this*."

"Listen, I've been thinking this over," said Miranda. "I bet this is all part of some game. You know how some dolls cry, or pee, or call you Mommy? Well, this one turns you into a zombie. It's supposed to be just for fun. "

"You think so?" Stanley asked.

"I'm sure of it," Miranda insisted. "And if I'm right, then there has to be some antidote that will turn Felicity back to normal once the game is over."

"Great!" Stanley said. "But how do we find out what it is?"

"Didn't the Widow say Zombiekins came with instructions? There must be something about the antidote in there."

Stanley gulped a piece of unchewed taffy down the wrong way.

"Um ... er ... yeah ... uhhhhhhh ... " he explained.

"Don't tell me you threw away the instructions? Oh, Stanley ... "

"How was I supposed to know it turned kids into insatiable monsters?"

Over at Felicity's table, Butch handed Kathleen something blue and hairy in a plastic bag.

"I found this at the back of my desk!" he announced. "I think it's from first term!"

Kathleen took the hairy blue sandwich from the bag and held it up with two fingers. Felicity craned forward like a baby bird and snatched it out of Kathleen's hand, accidentally nipping her finger, then gulped it down without chewing. (The sandwich, not the finger.)

"In that case," Miranda said, "I guess we just better hope we find Zombiekins before this gets any worse...."

23

**THE PLAYGROUND OF DEMENTEDYVILLE ELEMENTARY**
at a few minutes before noon was a quiet, peaceful place, where squirrels darted to and fro across the pavement and butterflies fluttered lazily in the midday sun.

That is, until the recess bell rang.

Then the squirrels took to the trees, the butterflies dipsy-doodled it out of there for all they were worth, and all along the neighboring street little old ladies puttering in rose gardens dropped their pruning shears and hurried indoors to safety.

Because the first peal of the recess bell touched off a rumbling inside the school that rose and swelled like a gathering flood....

. . . Until all at once a tidal wave of children burst into the yard, pouring from all the doors and spilling out of windows. Suddenly the air was loud with the joyful sounds of children laughing, children singing, children shouting rude names as they raced to be the first to claim the foursquare courts and swings and the topmost branches of the tree nobody was supposed to climb in.

Over at the tetherball court, a freckly-faced boy and a tall girl with braces arrived together and grabbed the ball at the same instant.

"I was first," said the freckly-faced boy, with a tug.

"No, I was first," said the tall girl, with a yank.

Behind them, a line was already forming; kids were pushing and shoving to get closer to the front.

But then a shadow falling across the tetherball court made everyone look up. . . .

The kids in line stopped jostling and stared with frightened eyes.... The tall girl let the tetherball slip through her hands and stepped back, shaking.... The freckly-faced boy let go too and backed away, quaking....

It was a pack of sixth graders—they always traveled in packs—and just the sight of them was enough to send the younger kids scurrying for cover. The boys wore black T-shirts, dark hoodies and permanent sneers, and their hair was an open rebellion against society and interfering mothers. The girls had improbable hair colors and makeup plastered on so thick they looked like ghoulish figures from a wax museum. Next to the kindergarteners, they were the scariest kids in the school.

One by one, all the children in line disappeared—except for one girl from third grade, who shuffled ahead as the line melted away until finally she stepped up and took hold of the tetherball.

"Hey, kid, are you blind or something?" said a sixth grader who looked like a gorilla. "We're playing with that."

"Yeah, twerp, are you deaf or something?" said another sixth grader who smelled like a baboon. "Beat it."

The girl turned slowly and stiffly to face them. It was Mackenzie. She growled from deep in her throat, like a dog: "*Grrrrrrrrrr ...*"

Gorilla Face and his friend with the baboon-fresh scent halted, like they didn't want to get any closer. But a couple of their classmates piped up behind them:

"Go play on the swings, pip-squeak," said a girl with blood-red fingernails.

"Yeah, go build a sand castle for your dollies, shrimp," said another girl with vampire-bat-black lips.

They shoved the boys from their class forward into Mackenzie—

And like a cornered animal, she snarled and lunged back at them.

"Ow! She *bit* me!" yelped Gorilla Face. "Great, now I'll probably have to get shots!"

**"ALL I'M SAYING IS, SOMETHING BAD MUST'VE** happened to Knuckles," Stanley said, lining up a free throw under the basketball net. "You know he wouldn't miss dodgeball for anything."

"Stanley, I'm telling you, this is all just some kind of game," Miranda said. "Zombiekins is still just a toy. Sure, it turns kids into zombies—but it wouldn't actually *hurt* them."

A burst of screaming from the direction of the tetherball court made Stanley flinch. His shot never reached the backboard.

"Oh, yeah?" Stanley said. "Look what it did to Felicity...."

"I don't know," said Miranda. "In some ways it's an improvement...."

"Yeah, but that's just from one little bite," Stanley said. "What if Knuckles didn't get away so easily? *What if . . .*" Stanley added, lowering his voice, ". . . *he didn't get away at all?*"

"Oh, stop letting your imagination get so carried away," Miranda scoffed.

Stanley aimed his next shot—but just as he was launching it, a bunch of kids ran in front of him, and the ball slipped from his hands in a weak arcing lob.

"Aaaaaaaaaahhhh!!!!" the kids screamed as they stampeded past.

Stanley turned to give a dirty look to whoever was chasing them . . .

...While his ball bounced limply off the backboard, rolled around the rim, then fainted through the hoop in exhaustion.

"*Nice shot!*" Miranda exclaimed.

But Stanley wasn't even looking. He was staring across the yard.

"The sixth g-g-graders..." he stammered. "They're ...they're ...*they're all zombies!*"

"How can you tell?" Miranda asked.

Sixth graders slouched and shuffled all over the playground, stiff-limbed, with pale, vacant faces and cold, lifeless eyes.

Speaking only in grunts or snarls, they trod on flowerbeds and barged through four-square games as though oblivious of their surroundings, attacking any kids who didn't get out of their way fast enough....

"So?" Miranda said. "They're always like that."

The recess bell rang. Instantly, the sixth graders stopped biting and mauling each other, lurched stiffly to attention, and started shuffling obediently into line by the door.

"Wonderful, Grade 6," Mrs. Plumdotty praised. "You're setting such a good example for the younger children."

Up and down the line, the sixth graders moaned and bellowed happily like petted dogs.

"You're right!" Miranda exclaimed. "They *are* a bunch of zombies!"

**AS THE SIXTH GRADERS TRUDGED UP THE STAIRS,**
a slow-moving line of growling, grumbling monsters,
all the younger children scattered from their path in
terror. Not because the other kids realized they were
zombies—just because they always stayed out of the
sixth graders' way.

"Oh, man," Stanley whimpered as he climbed
the stairs with Miranda. "I am in soooo much
trouble."

"Don't panic," Miranda said. "As long as it's just
the grade 6s, maybe no one will notice."

But an even bigger surprise was waiting for them
when they reached the third floor....

All of their classmates had been turned into zombies! They staggered mindlessly around the room,

bumping into desks and knocking over chairs. Sarah was licking the homework off the chalkboard. Carlos had his hand stuck in the pencil sharpener. Big Tony was sitting on the floor, mooing plaintively while zombie Fiona and zombie Kathleen whacked him with yardsticks.

Stanley and Miranda halted in the doorway, frozen with fear—terrified, that is, that their teacher would notice something out of the ordinary.

But when Mr. Baldengrumpy told the zombies to sit at their seats, they sat at their seats. When he told them to take out their books, they took out their books. And when he said, "Write your name at the top of the page," all the zombies tried to write "Your Name"—but between their zombie handwriting and zombie spelling, he never noticed.

In fact, for the rest of the period, as far as Mr. Baldengrumpy was concerned, the zombies were model students. They didn't speak without raising their hands. Or interrupt his lessons with pesky questions. Or finish their work so quickly he had to find something else for them to do.

Still, Stanley and Miranda thought they would be discovered for sure when Mr. Baldengrumpy called on Marcus to do his oral presentation on "Personal Hygiene in the Middle Ages."

Marcus stood at the front of the class, slumped and swaying like a barn door off its hinges. He was holding a poster the wrong way up and drooling down his shirtfront.

*"Ummm hrng grgl ummm glrrrdddll umm . . ."* he groaned.

*"Stop right there!"* Mr. Baldengrumpy barked.

Stanley felt a surge of panic. He was certain his teacher had noticed something wrong.

"Start again," Mr. Baldengrumpy ordered. "And do it without the 'um's this time."

Next to kids who walked up the wrong side of the stairwell, there was nothing Mr. Baldengrumpy hated more than mumbly public speakers.

Marcus just stared back blankly, wobbling and drooling.

*"Hrng grgl glrrdd ngghrrr . . ."* he moaned.

"Much better," said Mr. Baldengrumpy.

Halfway through the period, Miranda signaled Stanley to meet her at the back of the room.

"This is out of control," she said. "We've got to find Zombiekins and bring it back to the Widow after school. Maybe she can tell us what the antidote is."

"But we can't both leave class to go search," Stanley pointed out. "There's only one bathroom pass."

At that moment, their classmate Bryce came staggering down a nearby aisle carrying a pair of scissors, tripped over a kleenex and fell on his face. Slowly and clumsily, he dragged himself to his feet and looked around for the scissors—but he couldn't find them because they were stuck in his chest.

"Somehow I don't think that's the worst of our problems right now, Stanley," Miranda said.

**26**

**MIRANDA FIGURED THEY COULD SEARCH THE**
school faster if they split up, so she sent
Stanley to look in the
basement while she
combed the top
floors again. But
when he got down
there, the scene
that confronted
him stopped him
in his tracks. The
entrance to the
kindergarten
room was cov-
ered in blood-
red smears!

Terrified of what he'd find, Stanley had to force himself to look inside....

All over the classroom, little zombies in pigtails and short-pants were scratching, strangling, bashing, biting, mugging and mauling each other. There were kinderzombies in the sandbox, burying one another in sand ... kinderzombies

in the Story Corner, munching on their favorite books ... a crowd of kinderzombies clawing and drooling around a glass terrarium full of nervous caterpillars for the class butterfly project....

"Alice," Miss Mellow said in her usual calm honey tones, "we don't put Simon's head in our mouth."

In the middle of all this chaos, one little zombie stood patiently picking his nose—until a little girl zombie saw and lurched hungrily in his direction.

"*Mrhrnghrmdrn …*" the little girl zombie groaned, choking him.

"*MRGHNHRRGLLRR!*" the little boy zombie roared, choking her back.

"Use your inside voices," Miss Mellow gently reminded them.

Stanley backed out of the classroom in horror. Behind him, the hall was filled with a shrill, tuneless racket coming from down by the Music Room. It sounded like mice squealing, crows shrieking, geese quarreling, cows bellowing, donkeys braying, cats hissing, snakes yodeling, and a dog with its tail stuck in a door.

"Wonderful, children!" Stanley heard Mrs. Bernstein shouting from inside. "Louder!"

Stanley knew before he looked that it would be just like the kindergarten class. Sure enough, the room was full of zombies: zombies munching on ukuleles, zombies banging violins against their music stands like hammers, zombies blowing into the wrong ends of their trumpets—and none of them following the tune at all, except for one pair in the corner who were bashing each other over the head with cellos in time with Mrs. Bernstein's baton....

It was the same upstairs in the gym where the third graders were playing floor hockey. They swarmed around the ball, battering one another with  their sticks, while Mr. Straap stood on the sidelines shouting encouragements.

"Good hustle, Speckley," he called as a tall girl hacked her way through a pack of classmates.

Another boy stumbled after the ball, dragging a weirdly bent and twisted leg behind him.

"That's it, Puffler," Mr. Straap cheered. "Don't give up on the play!"

But then one of the zombies inadvertently scored a goal and play was stopped while the goalie fished the ball out of the back of the net and ate a chunk of it.

RIP
27

**BUT STANLEY AND MIRANDA DIDN'T FIND ANY SIGN**
of Zombiekins, and by the time they met up again at
last recess, the playground was swarming with zombies. Some were just staggering around, aimless and
vaguely menacing, like teenagers. Others were playing normal recess games—except their reflexes were
so slow they got tangled up in skipping ropes, and
games of catch turned into games of fetch, and every
serve in foursquare bounced off somebody's chest
and rolled across the yard out into traffic.

Stanley and Miranda were tossing a ball around by themselves at the back of the yard when two zombies stumbled through the flower garden beside them, choking and biting each other.

"Mind you don't trample the tulips, boys," tutted Mrs. Plumdotty.

"We have to tell her," Stanley said. "This is out of control."

"Tell her what? That you accidentally turned all the kids in school into zombies?" Miranda replied. "You'd be in detention till you're eighty."

Stanley noticed she didn't say "we."

"Let's just worry about finding Zombiekins for now," Miranda went on. "Then after school, we'll go ask the Widow about the antidote."

She tossed the ball lightly to Stanley, but it bounced through his legs and rolled away under the dumpster by the back fence.

"Don't worry," Stanley said reassuringly a moment later, lying on his stomach. "I see it."

It was dark and filthy as a cave under the dumpster but Stanley thought he could just make out a shadowy bump way at the back that might be a ball. He started to crawl under to get it. His head bumped against the bottom of the dumpster with a loud *thunk*!

*Ouch*! That smarted. Stanley shimmied forward, more carefully this time. But to his surprise the noise rang out again, like some strange, delayed echo: *thunk*!

And then again: *thunk*!

"Weird," Stanley mumbled, crawling further under.

Above him, there was a loud **skkkkrrrrrrrrkkkkk** like claws scratching on metal ... then a *creeeeeakkk* like the lid of a dumpster opening....

"Uhhh, Stanley ..." said Miranda.

"Hold on," Stanley replied, stretching as far as he could. "I've—almost— "

"Stanley, you really ought to—"

But Stanley didn't catch the rest of her remark because it was drowned out by a low, vowelless growl: "*Mngrbrgngnlll . . .*"

"Got it!" Stanley announced triumphantly, backing out from under the dumpster and rising to his feet. He dusted off his shirtfront and proudly held out the dirt-covered ball.

But Miranda didn't even give it a glance. She was staring right past Stanley, her eyes wide with terror and fixed on something just over his shoulder. . . .

Behind him, there was another growl: "*Mngrbrgngnlll . . .*"

This time Stanley started to turn around. . . .

Rising slowly from the dumpster behind him was Knuckles. Pale as a corpse, with cold dead eyes and wild matted hair, drooling garbage juice down his chin, he looked even more like a monster than usual.

When Knuckles recognized Stanley, his zombie eyes flashed with rage—or maybe it was hunger. He spat out a mouthful of garbage and growled again, more distinctly: *"Mnaarrhaarbwragnagnylll...."* Then, slowly and awkwardly, Knuckles started climbing out of the dumpster.

Too scared to run, Stanley could only watch in horror as Knuckles hoisted himself over the side of the dumpster with stiff, clumsy movements—then lost his balance—teetered on the edge—and fell headfirst on top of Stanley!

## 28

**"GET HIM OFF ME!" STANLEY BEGGED MIRANDA. "HE'S** trying to kill me!"

Actually, Knuckles was sprawled motionless on his back on top of Stanley as though the fall had stunned him. But when Stanley started to squirm out from under him, Knuckles grabbed Stanley's leg.

"Don't let him intimidate you, Stanley," Miranda said. "This is your chance to stand up to him!"

But Stanley was in no position to stand up to anyone at that particular moment because Knuckles was dangling him off the ground by an ankle.

"Go on, Stanley, show him he can't push you around," Miranda urged as Knuckles pushed Stanley around, then pummeled him about, then ping-ponged him to and fro.

"Hellllllllllp!" Stanley pleaded as Knuckles twirled him around and around. "Doooo somethinggggg!"

Miranda just shook her head.

"Okay," she said in a disappointed voice. "Keep him busy till I get back."

So Stanley kept Knuckles busy. First he seized hold of Knuckles' hand with his neck. Then he pounded Knuckles in the fist with his face. Then he bashed Knuckles in the knee with the side of his head.

Stanley was just lying down on the pavement to strike Knuckles sharply and repeatedly in the foot with his stomach when Miranda reappeared with a wooden baseball bat.

"What are you wait-ait-aiting for-or-or?" Stanley pleaded as Knuckles shook him upside down like someone trying to squeeze the last drop out of a ketchup bottle. "Hit him-im-im!"

"No, Stanley," Miranda said. "You have to be the one to do it. He'll never leave you alone until you show him you can stick up for yourself."

Knuckles flipped Stanley high in the air like a coin and Stanley slammed down on the pavement on his back. Taffy spilled from his backpack like a splatter of guts.

"You'll thank me for this later," Miranda insisted. "That is, unless...."

She trailed off without finishing, and with a little shrug, threw the bat to Stanley.

Before Knuckles could pick him up for another toss, Stanley sprang to his feet and backed away with it cocked over his shoulder.

"Stay back," Stanley warned. "I mean it."

Knuckles just kept staggering toward him, snarling and drooling and snapping his jaws in hungry chomping motions.

"Aim for the head," said Miranda. "It's the only way to stop a zombie."

Stanley's fingers tightened around the bat handle....

"Do it, Stanley," Miranda urged. "He's not Knuckles anymore...."

But Stanley just let the bat fall to his side. He couldn't do it.

And the next moment, Knuckles grabbed Stanley around the neck and started pulling him closer with his mouth stretched wide....

"Don't let him bite you!" Miranda shouted. "You'll be turned into a zombie!"

Stanley fought and squirmed, but Knuckles' grip was like iron ... His teeth were inches from Stanley's neck....

With his last drop of strength, Stanley swung the bat—

And with a loud *crack!*, it splintered against the side of Knuckles' head!

"Now, boys," Mrs. Plumdotty tutted. "Use words, not sticks."

Knuckles wobbled backward, holding his temples like someone with a splitting headache. He staggered to a halt in front of the swings. He growled at Stanley with eyes full of hate, bared his teeth, and lurched forward....

Into the path of a zombie swooping down on the swings!

Knuckles was knocked backwards—toward the roundabout, which a couple other zombies were steadily and robotically spinning.

Knuckles' belt loop caught on the roundabout, and like someone sucked into a tornado, he spun around, and around, and around....

"Ouch!" Stanley winced. *"Turbo wedgie."*

Stanley started sweeping the Widow's taffy back into his knapsack

"Did you see that?" Stanley bragged to Miranda. "That'll teach *him* to pick on Stanley Nudelman!"

"Uh-oh . . ." Miranda said beside him.

"'Uh-oh' what?" asked Stanley, looking up.

"Uh-oh *that*—"

159

**29**

**THEY WERE SURROUNDED**
by an army of zombies. A
sea of zombies. Or a bunch
of them, anyway. All staring
at Stanley with blank, hungry
looks.

"*Hrnrgrghnrr,*" remarked
one of the zombies.

"*Yarrghhhh,*" commented another.

Then the whole crowd started *hrrgnghrr*ing and
*yaargh*ing—and suddenly they all surged forward,
snapping their jaws like hungry nestlings fighting
over a worm.

Stanley was cornered.

"The slide!" Miranda called to him
from the other side of the mob.

160

Zombies came grunting and groping, groaning and moaning, snapping and snarling toward Stanley on every side, closing in around him with their awful zombie eyes and their even awfuler zombie breath....

Stanley started to back away and bumped up against the play structure—trapped!

He was zombie food. A Stanley sandwich. A lunch buffet for the walking dead. A—

Wait a minute.... What was Miranda doing on the *other* side of the mob?

"Use the slide," she repeated calmly. "Just climb up and escape down the slide."

In a flash, Stanley understood. Well, maybe it took a couple of flashes. Actually, maybe it was more like when you're trying and trying to take a photograph and finally somebody points out that you forgot to turn the flash *on*. But eventually Stanley figured it out; that's the important thing.

He spun around and started scrambling up the crisscrossing

ropes behind him. Zombies clutched and clawed at his legs, stretching their mouths to chomp into them like drumsticks. One got hold of his shoelace and started pulling Stanley back down with the strength of ten fourth graders. The mob below let out a hungry moan as Stanley slipped—back—toward them—

Luckily, his shoelace came untied and slid through the zombie's grasp. (Good thing he was never very good at tying double knots.) And with the last of his strength, Stanley pulled himself to safety.

Stanley shimmied along a wooden beam toward the slide. A few of the zombies tried to follow him up the rope ladder but got tangled like fish in a net. The rest were so slow-moving and slow-thinking that by the time they caught on what Stanley was doing, he had swooped down the slide to join Miranda.

But the two of them weren't out of trouble yet. They were still trapped in a playground full of zombies, cut off from the only gate leading out of the yard. And it wasn't long before the crowd under the play structure realized they'd been duped and came stumbling and staggering after them, moaning angrily.

Stanley and Miranda made a dash for the back door with the angry zombie mob right on their tail. Stanley barely had time to stop and tie his shoelace....

They reached the back door just as the recess bell rang....

"It's locked!" Miranda cried.

**STANLEY YANKED AND**
yanked on the handle, but
it was no use. He pounded
on the door, but there was
nobody inside to hear. . . .

"I sent Russell in to open
it," Mrs. Plumdotty said cheer-
fully, appearing beside them. "I
wonder what's keeping him. I do
hope he isn't dawdling."

By now every zombie in the whole
playground was schlepping and schlumphing
toward them—some chasing Stanley and Miranda,
the rest just obediently staggering into line by
the door.

"Mrs. Plumdotty, we have to get out of here!" Miranda blurted out. "These kids are all zombies!"

Stanley's heart sank. He knew they must be in bad trouble if Miranda was asking for help from a teacher.

"Now, Miranda," Mrs. Plumdotty replied, "you know it's not nice to call the other children names."

"No, you don't understand," Stanley hurried to explain. "She means they're flesh-eating monsters who want to guzzle our livers and gobble our limbs!"

"Stanley, dear, don't be such a tattletale," chided Mrs. Plumdotty.

Stanley and Miranda stood with their backs against the school wall, completely surrounded by moaning, groaning, grasping, grumbling zombies....

Suddenly the door beside them swung open and a little zombie stumbled out.

"*Hhrngghrghrgllng...*" the zombie groaned mindlessly.

"Thank you, Russell, dear," Mrs. Plumdotty said.

And before the door could swing closed again, Stanley and Miranda ducked under a swarm of grasping zombie arms and dashed inside.

"Wait, dears!" Mrs. Plumdotty called after them. "I haven't sent your line in yet."

But Stanley and Miranda bolted up the stairs, not thinking where they were headed, just trying to put as much distance as possible between themselves and the horde of zombies already filing into the stairwell behind them....

They reached the second floor landing, wheeled around without stopping, dashed up to the—

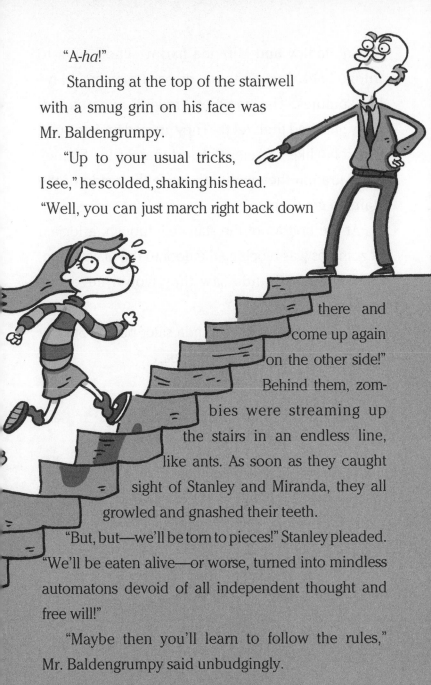

"A-*ha*!"

Standing at the top of the stairwell with a smug grin on his face was Mr. Baldengrumpy.

"Up to your usual tricks, I see," he scolded, shaking his head. "Well, you can just march right back down there and come up again on the other side!" Behind them, zombies were streaming up the stairs in an endless line, like ants. As soon as they caught sight of Stanley and Miranda, they all growled and gnashed their teeth.

"But, but—we'll be torn to pieces!" Stanley pleaded. "We'll be eaten alive—or worse, turned into mindless automatons devoid of all independent thought and free will!"

"Maybe then you'll learn to follow the rules," Mr. Baldengrumpy said unbudgingly.

So Stanley and Miranda had no choice but to trudge back down into the mass of mawing, clawing zombies. The zombies growled and snarled. They gnashed their teeth. They groped and grasped with clawlike fingers. But fortunately for Stanley and Miranda they wouldn't leave their side of the stairs to get them.

At the bottom of the stairwell, though, a logjam of zombies was blocking the door to the playground. Stanley and Miranda saw they would never get through.

"Quick—this way!" Miranda said, pulling Stanley back up the stairs. "I have an idea...."

The second-floor hallway, where the primary classrooms were, was crawling with zombie first graders and zombie second graders. Pale as corpses, with dead soulless eyes and mouths full of dark yawning gaps where they'd lost their baby teeth, they were a terrifying sight—or might have been, except that the tallest of them barely came up to Stanley's shoulder.

Stanley and Miranda burst into the hall. For a moment, the first and second graders just stopped and stared. Then, with a great howl, they all set upon Stanley and Miranda like a pack of wild dogs—small ones, jumping up on them and nipping at their elbows.

Stanley and Miranda fought their way through the mob, made a dash toward the heavy fire doors at the end of the hall, and escaped while all the grade 1s and 2s stopped to change into their indoor shoes like good little zombies.

Beyond the doors, the hall branched off to the right, and Stanley followed Miranda past the Library, the Computer Lab....

"Where are we going?" he asked. "This hallway is a dead end."

"Not exactly," Miranda said, stopping in front of the door at the end of the hall. "Come on, they'll never think to look for us in here."

"Oh, no . . ." Stanley hesitated. "Not there . . . We can't...."

They heard the fire doors open behind them and a stampede of shuffling footsteps approaching around the corner. Miranda shoved Stanley through the door and slammed it shut behind them. . . .

**"QUICK!" MIRANDA SAID. "HELP ME MOVE THIS SOFA."**

Together they dragged a ratty old sofa across the room and pushed it up against the door. Then they piled everything they could find on top of it: stacks of vacation catalogs, huge dusty piles of unmarked homework they uncovered when they moved the sofa, all the furniture in the room that wasn't too heavy to move....

"Ew," said Stanley, "there's chewing gum stuck under all these chairs."

On the other side of the door, the noise kept building until it sounded like there was a stampede of angry cattle mooing and mulling out in the hall.

Stanley and Miranda took cover behind a table at the back of the room as the clamor reached its peak. The zombies were right outside the door!

"*Mmmhhrrgh!*" roared one of them.

"*Nnyyyarrrghrggl!*" raged another.

There was a pause.

"*Mrrghhr?*" groaned another zombie, more puzzled than angry.

Stanley held his breath, hoping they would give up looking and go away. But the next moment, the sound of the door handle jiggling made his blood freeze—they were trying to get in!

One of them started pounding on the door...

Then another...

and another...

Until soon the door shook with a thunder of thumping and battering that rattled all the junk heaped against it and stirred up a dust cloud from the pile of unmarked homework...

But their barricade held.

After a few tense moments, the pounding stopped. Gradually the angry voices dimmed. There was a shuffling of feet outside in the hall, then that too fell silent.

"I think they've gone back to class," Miranda whispered.

"Phew!" Stanley sighed. "Now let's get out of here and go ask the Widow for help."

"No, hold on," Miranda said. "I think we should wait here till school is over and they've all gone home."

Stanley started to object, but Miranda explained:

"It's the perfect hideout," she went on. "In all the zombie movies I've ever seen, the heroes always hole up somewhere just like this. Somewhere with only one way in, where you'd never expect the zombies to find them...."

"But what if they *do* find us?" Stanley asked. "Doesn't that mean there's only one way *out*, too?"

"Oh, they always find you," Miranda said, matter-of-factly. "But trust me, this is just the way it's done."

Stanley couldn't argue with her. He never watched

scary movies because they made him see monsters in the shadows cast by his nightlight for weeks after.

So they tried to relax and look for ways to pass the time until school was over. Miranda went around checking the windows for an escape route, but they'd all been sealed shut to prevent teachers from climbing out onto the ledge on rainy days when the children were kept indoors for recess.

As for Stanley, now that he wasn't being chased by flesh-eating zombies, he realized he was pretty hungry himself. He never did get a proper lunch, after all. But even though the Teacher's Lounge was full of old pizza boxes and empty glasses with little umbrellas in them, he couldn't find a crumb of anything to eat. Finally he got so desperate he decided to eat some of the Widow's taffy from his knapsack.

"Hey," Stanley said, peeling the wrapper off a piece of taffy with a loud *mmmmmmrip*, "how come we never thought to look for Zombiekins in here?"

As soon as the words left Stanley's mouth, an awful thought struck him. He tried to push it out of his mind— but he could tell by the way Miranda was staring back at him that the same idea had just occurred to her....

And then, from somewhere nearby in the room, with timing so pat it was downright eerie, they heard it:

**Stump!—scri-i-i-i-i-itch**...

From out of a broom closet by the door, Zombiekins appeared....

**Stump!—scri-i-i-i-i-itch**...

Slowly but steadily, Zombiekins advanced across the room toward them, one leg dragging like a dead limb....

**Stump!—scri-i-i-i-itch** . . .

Slowly but steadily, it came bearing down on Stanley and Miranda like some monster out of a horror movie. . . .

... Like some really short monster ... Which also happened to be really slow ...

But it wasn't long (well, not *that* long, anyway) before Zombiekins had crossed the room and was almost upon them.

Fortunately Stanley and Miranda managed to escape in the nick of time by taking a couple steps backward.

"W-what should we do?" Stanley asked Miranda.

"Catch it in your knapsack," Miranda said, inching back another step.

That had been their plan all along—but it didn't seem so easy now that they found themselves trapped in a room with a killer teddy.

Zombiekins just kept dragging itself steadily after them, and Stanley and Miranda kept edging away, and edging away, until finally on their third lap around the room Miranda made a suggestion.

"On second thought," she said, "maybe we *should* sneak out of school while the zombies are stuck in class...."

They made a dash across the room and started digging through the barricade, item by item.

Zombiekins turned and followed them, slowly and menacingly....

**Stump!—scri-i-i-i-i-itch** ...

"It's following us slowly and menacingly!" Stanley said.

They lifted chairs off the pile as fast as they could. Soon Zombiekins was just a few steps away.

**Stump!—scri-i-i-i-i-itch** ...

"It's just a few steps away!" Stanley shrieked.

"Don't panic!" Miranda said in a panicky voice, as she pushed the sofa aside and swung the door open—

"*Now* panic?" asked Stanley.

"Okay," Miranda muttered in shock. "I guess now you may as well go ahead and panic...."

**FOR ONE TENSE MOMENT, STANLEY AND MIRANDA**
stared out at the mob staring in at them. Then, slowly,
a flicker of understanding spread through the crowd—
and with a sudden roar, all the zombies surged forward
at once!

Miranda tried to slam the door, but it caught with
a loud crunch of bone—a zombie at the front had
jammed its arm in the crack!

"Quick," Miranda gasped, leaning into the door
with all her might, "push the sofa back!"

Stanley did, then together they quickly piled the
stacks of vacation catalogues and unmarked homework back on top. But already more grasping arms
were writhing over the threshold, and Stanley and
Miranda could see it was only a matter of time before
their barricade gave way....

183

184

Then their barricade gave way.

There was a mighty push from the other side and the door flung open, toppling the sofa and sending holiday catalogues and unmarked math tests fluttering all over the room.

Stanley and Miranda backed away in helpless terror. There was nothing between them and the mob of bloodthirsty zombies now....

Except that all the zombies tried to push through the doorway at once and got stuck.

It wasn't long, though, before they started squeezing one by one into the room. Soon they were closing in around Stanley and Miranda on all sides. Their eyes were blank and clouded over, their skin was gray and clammy—and, collectively, they really could've used a breath mint.

Backed against the far wall, Stanley and Miranda looked around desperately for some weapon to fend the zombies off with. But there was nothing. Then Miranda's glance fell on the piece of unwrapped taffy Stanley was still holding and a strange look came into her eye.

"Hey, what if..." she muttered to herself, as if an idea had just occurred to her. "Quick, Stanley, give me your knapsack!"

Stanley passed it to her, thinking she was going to swing it at the zombies. Instead, she plunged her hand inside and brought out a handful of the Widow's taffy.

"Try throwing this at them," she said, tossing the knapsack back. "I have a hunch it might slow them down...."

She wound up and hit the first zombie square between the eyes. The zombie didn't even flinch, and the candy bounced harmlessly to the floor.

Stanley thought Miranda was crazy, but she wouldn't give up. She just kept pelting the oncoming hordes with taffy, hitting one zombie after another.

Meanwhile, the first zombie stopped and stared

at the taffy lying at its feet. Slowly, he bent forward, picked it up, and tore the wrapper off with clumsy fingers. He stood for a moment gawking at the hard brown lump—then popped it into his mouth.

There was a crack and crunch of breaking teeth as the zombie chewed....

And chewww-wwwed...

And chewww-wwww-wwww-www-wwwwed...

Miranda was right—the Widow's taffy *was* slowing him down!

All around the room, other zombies had stopped to pounce on the candy. Some started fighting over it, bashing and choking each other for a piece.

Whatever Miranda's plan was, Stanley thought, it looked like it was working—at least for the moment.

He dug some more taffy out of his knapsack and started flinging the stuff like mad along with her.

But then, from out of the crowd of wrangling-strangling-biting-fighting-smashing-bashing zombies came Zombiekins itself, staggering toward them....

Stanley and Miranda shrank back in terror.

"Oh, no!" Miranda said. "Just when it looked like we might make it after all...."

The note of hopelessness in her voice gave Stanley a chill. Miranda was the one who always bailed them out of jams—if she was giving up, they were done for.

At least, that was the first thought to pass through Stanley's mind. But the next moment, it was as if a strange change came over him. Maybe it was that everything he had been through that day had stirred something unsuspected deep inside him. Or maybe it was just that even a boy like Stanley can be pushed only so far.

But whatever it was, Stanley puffed his chest out in a superhero pose and stepped out from behind Miranda.

"Cover me," he said, his voice straining a little from the effort of flexing his chest. "I'm going to catch it in my knapsack."

Miranda stared at Stanley in surprise. For as long as she had known him, he had always been the kind of boy who didn't like taking chances. Now, suddenly, he was like some brave new Stanley Nudelman.

And the new Stanley Nudelman puffed his chest out some more and leaped fearlessly over the barricade....

Unfortunately the new Stanley caught his foot on the table edge and landed with a faceplant on the other side. The knapsack slipped from his hands and the rest of the Widow's taffy skittered away across the floor.

He peeled his face up off the floor to see the teddy of terror inching toward him. . . .

**Stump!—scri-i-i-i-i-itch** . . . **Stump!—scri-i-i-i-i-itch** . . . **Stump!—scri-i-i-i-i-itch** . . .

And the new Stanley Nudelman did the only thing he could think of under the circumstances. He bravely squeezed his eyes shut and screamed like a baby:

"Waaaaaaaaaaahhhhhhhhhh—"

**33**

**"—AAAAHHHHHHH—"**

Stanley went on and on screaming as something was shaking him, and shaking him....

"—aaahhhhhunnnnhhh?"

Stanley peeked out with one eye. It wasn't Zombiekins shaking him, just Miranda.

Zombiekins, actually, had halted a few inches from Stanley's nose to nibble a piece of the Widow's taffy off the floor. Its fierce fangs made short work of the cement-like candy, devouring it without a trace in seconds, and Stanley trembled at such a terrifying display of lethal power.

But instead of coming after Stanley when it had finished, Zombiekins just uttered a happy little moan, sat back on its teddy-bear haunches, and closed its eyes like a smiling baby. Then it appeared to go to sleep.

Laying there, still and sleeping, Zombiekins looked peaceful and not-at-all-bloodthirsty. As if it was nothing but a harmless stuffy after all—in spite of its somewhat macabre, half-dead appearance.

Miranda gave Stanley another shake and he looked up. All over the room, the other zombies had stopped advancing and were standing around, chewing intently. The Widow's taffy had halted them in their tracks!

Then something even more incredible happened. The first zombie began to twitch and jerk. . . . It shivered with strange convulsions . . . It bent forward, clutching its hands to its face . . .

. . . And when the zombie straightened up again, he was Sasha Govay, no more terrifying or undead than your average fourth grader.

Sasha stared around him with a blank, confused look, like someone waking from a deep sleep.

Behind his back, the other zombies had started twitching and jerking too. . . .

"W-what's happening?" Stanley asked, with a blank, confused look of his own.

"It was the taffy!" Miranda said. "You had the antidote in your knapsack all along, doofus!"

"How did you figure it out?" Stanley asked.

"I remembered what the Widow said when she gave it to you," Miranda explained. "'*You never know when it might come in handy....*'"

But any relief Stanley and Miranda might have felt at being spared from having their limbs ripped off by zombies didn't last long. Because as soon as the other kids had turned back to normal, they started asking questions. Very uncomfortable questions. Questions like "Where are we?" and "How did we get here?" and "Why does Bryce have a pair of scissors stuck in his chest?"

There was a heavy silence as everyone stared at the scissors jutting out of Bryce's chest. Talk about awkward.

Luckily, at just that moment, someone at the back yelled, "Teachers coming! Everybody hide!"

Kids scurried for cover like ants. Just as the last of them were squeezing into cupboards or behind curtains, Mr. Straap and Ms. Mellow appeared in the doorway.

But Stanley saw at once they weren't themselves: Mr. Straap staggered stiffly and awkwardly, with no more athletic coordination than an alligator on roller skates. And sweet-tempered Ms. Mellow gnashed her teeth and snarled with honey-toned strangled gurgling noises....

As soon as the zombified teachers saw Stanley and Miranda, their eyes flashed with a fierce blood-thirsty gleam and they came drooling toward them like hungry wolves ... Zombie Ms. Mellow snarled sweetly ... Zombie Mr. Straap stumbled over a bump in the carpet. ...

Behind their backs, kids slipped from their hiding places and tiptoed out into the hall.

"We're dead!" Stanley squeaked.

"Relax," Miranda whispered. "We have the antidote, remember?"

She dangled two pieces of the Widow's taffy in front of her, and Mr. Straap and Ms. Mellow froze and sniffed the air like dogs.

"*Stayyyyyy*. ..." Miranda ordered. Ms. Mellow and Mr. Straap obeyed, ogling the taffy with tongues lolling out of their mouths.

Miranda tossed the taffy at their feet, and while the teachers pounced on the candy and devoured it like piranhas with a sweet tooth, she and Stanley ducked down behind an upturned table.

Within moments, the antidote started to take effect: The zombified teachers shivered, quivered, then popped back to normal.

Suddenly themselves again, Mr. Straap and Ms. Mellow stared around them in bewilderment at the wreckage of the staff room. For a moment, the two of them looked guilty as cornered criminals. Then, realizing they were alone, they relaxed a little, and a strange new look came over them....

Mr. Straap gazed into Ms. Mellow's eyes and sighed, "Oh, Marsha!"

And Ms. Mellow goggled him back and whimpered, "Oh, Jacques!"

Then Mr. Straap swept Ms. Mellow up in his arms, and she hefted him in hers, and their lips met in a kiss.

Crouched behind their upturned table, Stanley and Miranda winced and averted their eyes.

"Ewwww!" Stanley shuddered. "Now *that* was scary."

**34**

**STANLEY AND MIRANDA HAD NO TROUBLE SNEAKING** out of the staff room past Mr. Straap and Ms. Mellow. But out in the halls, they soon discovered their problems weren't over yet. In classroom after classroom, half the kids were still zombies—and in a few minutes, school would be over and they would all scatter to their homes.

"What can we do?" Stanley asked. "We'll never sneak the antidote to all these kids without getting caught."

And as long as there was one zombie left, it meant the whole plague could start all over again.

Fortunately, Miranda had a plan. She led Stanley down the stairwell to the playground door—the door where all the kids would exit at home time.

They didn't have to wait long. Almost as soon as the bell rang, the stairwell started to shake and rumble as if they were in the middle of an earthquake. Suddenly a stampede of children came barging, charging,

199

rushing, racing, hustling, hurtling down the stairs, leaping three steps at a time, sliding down the handrails, shoving, jostling, dashing, darting, whooping, hollering, barreling, bounding, bustling, and finally bursting through the playground doors to freedom.

Just as suddenly, all the kids were gone and the stairwell fell silent.

Then came the zombies. A long procession, filing down the stairs in a slow, orderly manner. None of them hurrying, none of them yelling, none of them pushing or trying to budge each other in line.

At the sight of Stanley and Miranda, they growled and snarled and licked their zombie chops.

But Stanley and Miranda just lured them through the door and fed them taffy on the other side. A few minutes later, the playground was full of kids scratching their heads, and there wasn't a zombie in sight.

Walking home, Stanley and Miranda talked about what to do with Zombiekins.

"You have to give it back to the Widow," Miranda urged. "As long as you don't know what made it come to life, you never know when this zombie mayhem might start up all over again."

"I guess you're right," Stanley said glumly. "But I was really starting to like the little guy...."

He gazed fondly at Zombiekins. It was actually kind of cute—in a macabre, half-dead way.

Miranda was the one who noticed the wedge of cardboard sticking out of a shrub by the edge of the sidewalk.

"Hey, look," she said in surprise. "It's Zombiekins' box—and the instructions are still in it."

"Weird," Stanley said. "I'm sure I threw that in a trash can. How could it have gotten here?"

**35**

THE NEXT DAY AT SCHOOL, IT WAS AS IF NOTHING had happened. All the kids were back to normal again, except Felicity was off with a stomachache and Knuckles had developed a phobia of stuffed animals and dollies.

After school, Stanley hurried straight home. Fetch met him at the door, barking and tugging on Stanley's shirt in a panicky way.

"Hi, Stanley," Baby Rosalie called from the playroom. "Want to play tea party with me?"

But Stanley ignored them both and headed for his room. He had something he needed to do.

Fetch jumped in front of Stanley, barring his way, making desperate gestures and pointing down the hall toward the playroom. When Stanley reached to open his bedroom door, Fetch flung himself around Stanley's feet with a pleading yowl.

"Not now, boy," Stanley said. "I'm too busy to take you for a walk."

He pushed Fetch aside and opened the door.

Fetch hid whining and whimpering under the bed as Stanley unlocked his closet with a key from under his pillow, lifted a metal box down from the top shelf, then opened it with another key he shook out of his piggy bank.

Inside the metal box was another box, all covered over with tape. As Stanley lifted it out, Fetch let out

a pathetic yowl and scurried away into the hall dribbling a trail of pee.

Stanley was relieved to find Zombiekins still in its box. Of course, the instructions said it would remain a harmless stuffy as long as it wasn't exposed to direct moonlight—but Stanley was not the kind of boy who liked taking chances. He fingered the taffy hanging from a string around his neck as he locked Zombiekins back up in the metal box in his closet. On his way out of the room, he tripped over an empty box by his bed, but didn't think anything of it.

In the toy room down the hall, meanwhile, Rosalie was playing tea party with her favorite stuffies.

There was a chair for Benny the Dinosaur and another chair for his head. Whimsy was sitting in a pool of his own stuffing and Schlemmo, looking like he had been ripped apart and not-too-expertly put back together again, was propped up in a chair with ropes. While Rosalie pretended to pour the tea, one of Schlemmo's arms fell off and plopped onto his saucer.

"Bad Schlemmo!" Rosalie scolded. "Elbows off the table."

It was getting dark and the moon was climbing the sky outside the playroom window by the time Rosalie's mother finally called her to bed. After that, it wasn't long before Stanley and his family were all sound asleep—except for Fetch, who spent the night pacing the upstairs hall.

Outside, the night was still and the little town of Dementedyville was once again the quiet, uneventful place it always had been. The sort of place where nothing exciting or out of the ordinary ever happened. And now that Zombiekins was safely locked up in Stanley's closet, that was how it would probably stay.

*Probably....*

**KEVIN BOLGER** is a writer and elementary reading teacher. *Sir Fartsalot Hunts the Booger* and *Zombiekins* were his first books for middle graders, and he is also the author of *See Fred Run* and other titles for beginner readers. He lives with his son in Ottawa, Canada.

**AARON BLECHA** was raised by a school of giant squids in Wisconsin and now lives with his wife in London, England. He works as an artist and animator, designing toys, making cartoons, and illustrating books, including the George Brown, Class Clown series. You can enjoy more of his twisted creations at **www.monstersquid.com**.

Thanks to Kristin Smith, Penguin book designer and honorary zombie, for her inspired page designs.

And to our editor, Jessica Rothenberg, for her infinite patience and unflagging support.